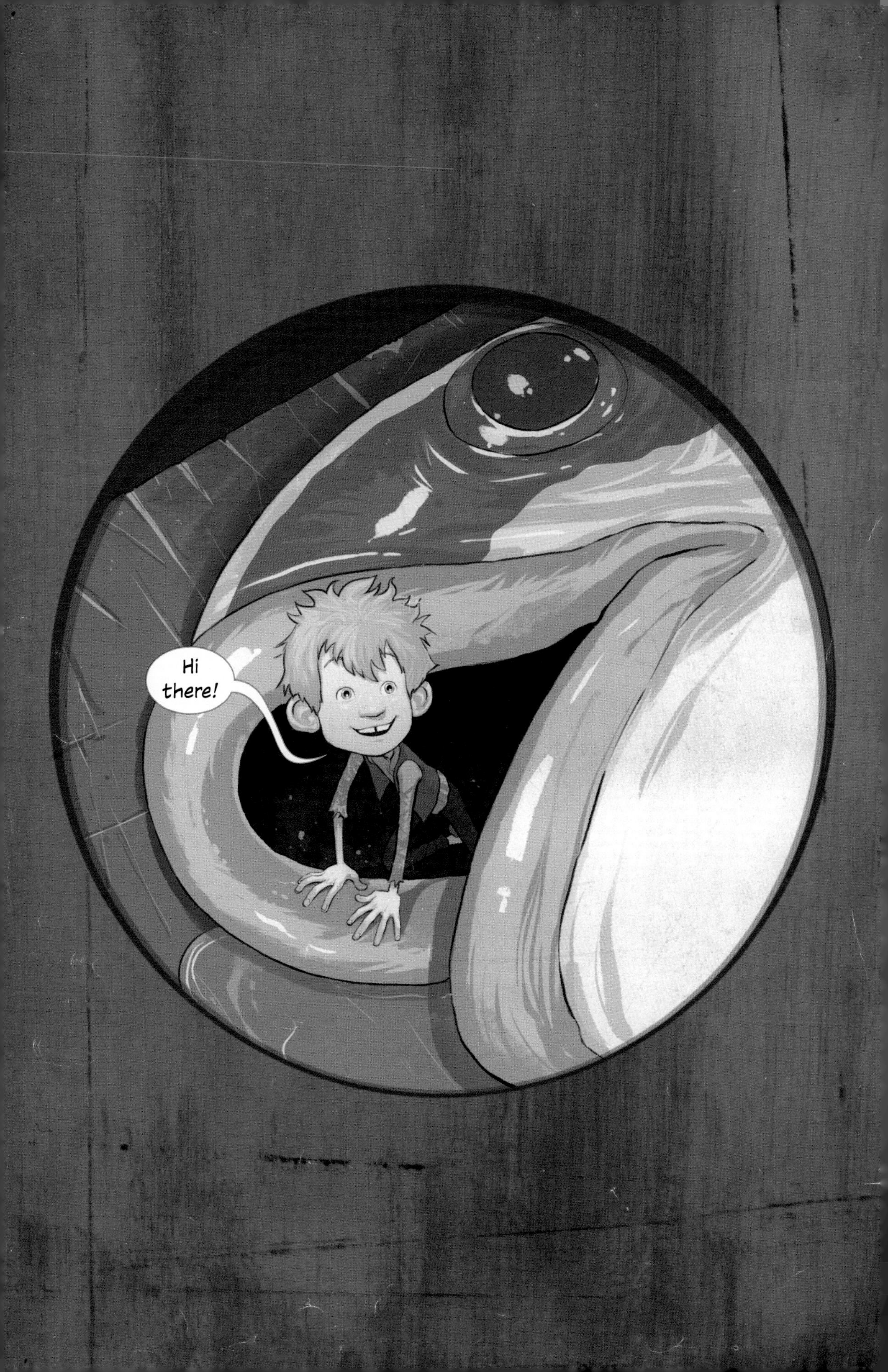
Hi there!

Graphic Spin is published by Stone Arch Books
A Capstone Imprint
151 Good Counsel Drive, P.O. Box 669
Mankato, Minnesota 56002
www.capstonepub.com

Library of Congress Cataloging-in-Publication Data
Sonneborn, Scott.
Tom Thumb : a Grimm graphic novel / retold by Scott Sonneborn ; illustrated by Nelson Evergreen.
p. cm. -- (Graphic spin)
ISBN 978-1-4342-2519-1 (library binding)
1. Graphic novels. [1. Graphic novels. 2. Fairy tales. 3. Folklore--England.] I. Grimm, Jacob, 1785-1863, II.
Grimm, Wilhelm, 1786-1859. III. Evergreen, Nelson, 1971- ill. IV. Tom Thumb. English. V. Title.
PZ7.7.S646To 2011
741.5'973--dc22
2010025337

Graphic Designer: Hilary Wacholz | Art Director: Kay Fraser

Summary: Being no larger than a thumb means tiny Tom must face big threats on a daily basis — even within
the confines of his loving parents' cozy home. Tom's plucky fearlessness and his thirst for adventure help him
outmaneuver hungry house cats and dodge deadly morsels of falling food with ease. But Tom's life is turned
upside down when he leaves the relative safety of his parents' house and enters the wide world outside!
Lost and alone, Tom Thumb will have to overcome colossal dangers to survive his perilous journey home.

Printed in the United States of America in North Mankato, Minnesota.
092010
005933CGS11

A GRIMM GRAPHIC NOVEL

TOM THUMB

WITHDRAWN

retold by Scott Sonneborn

illustrated by Nelson Evergreen

STONE ARCH BOOKS
a capstone imprint

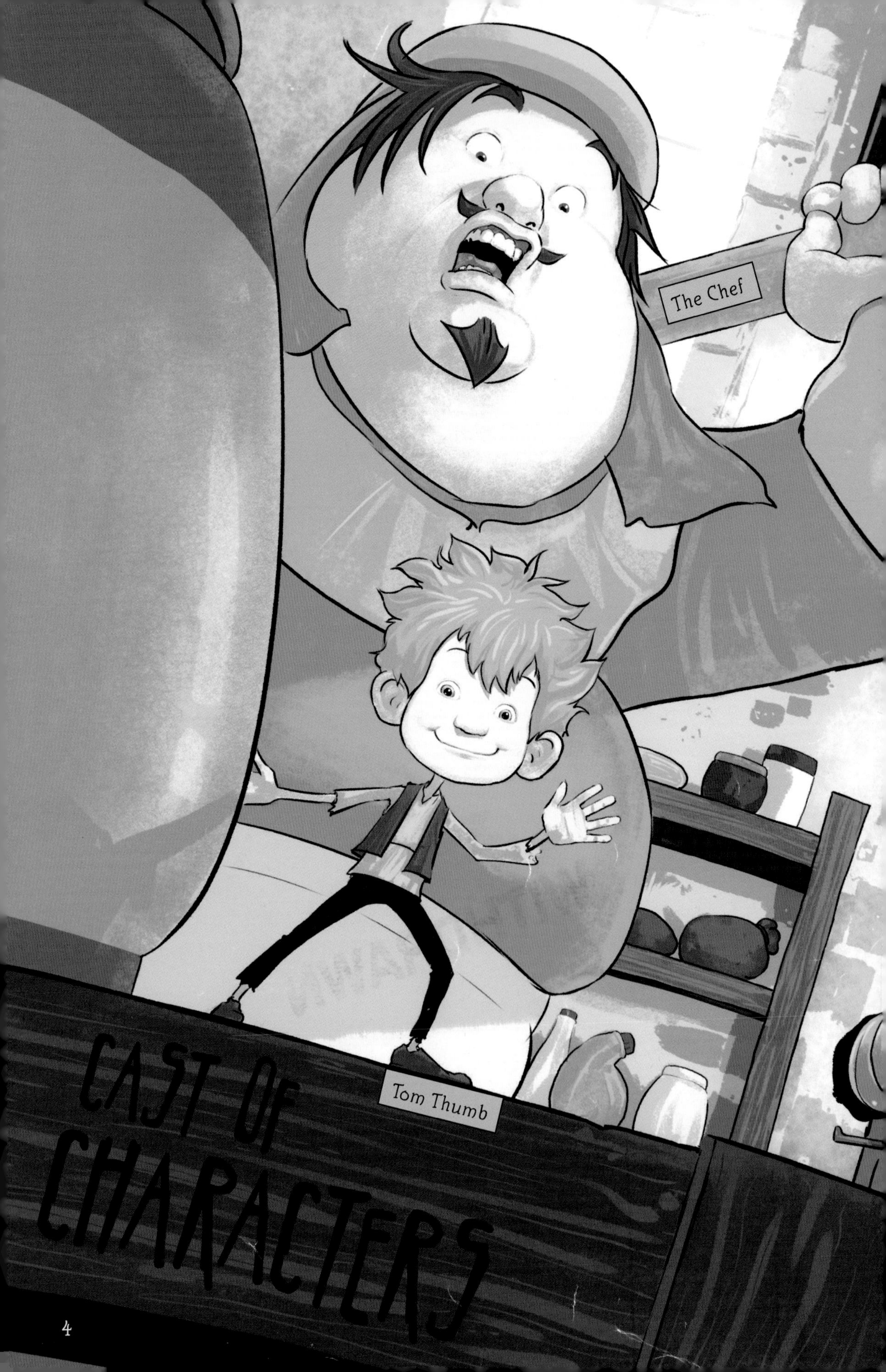
The Chef
Tom Thumb
CAST OF CHARACTERS

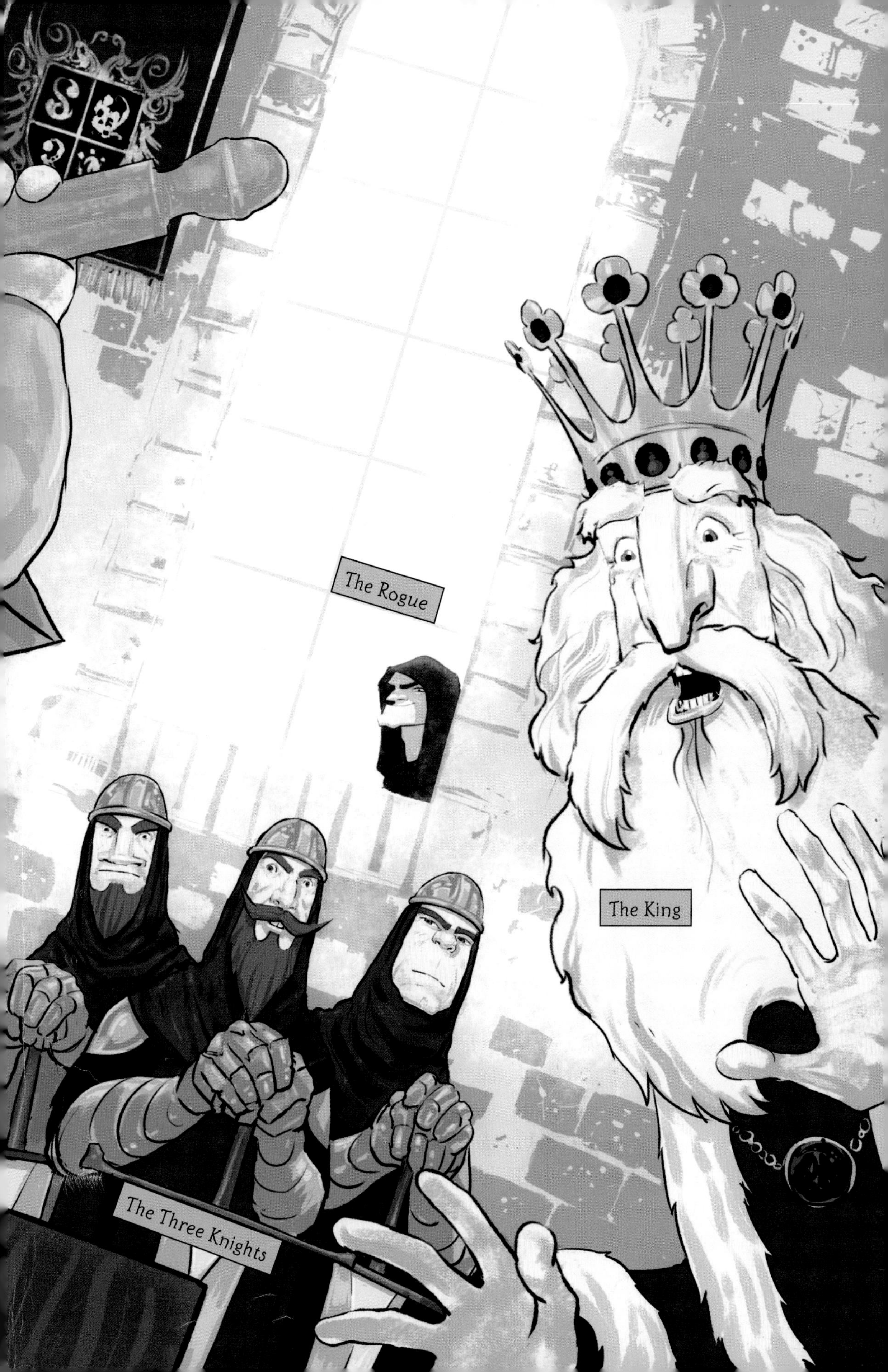
The Rogue
The King
The Three Knights

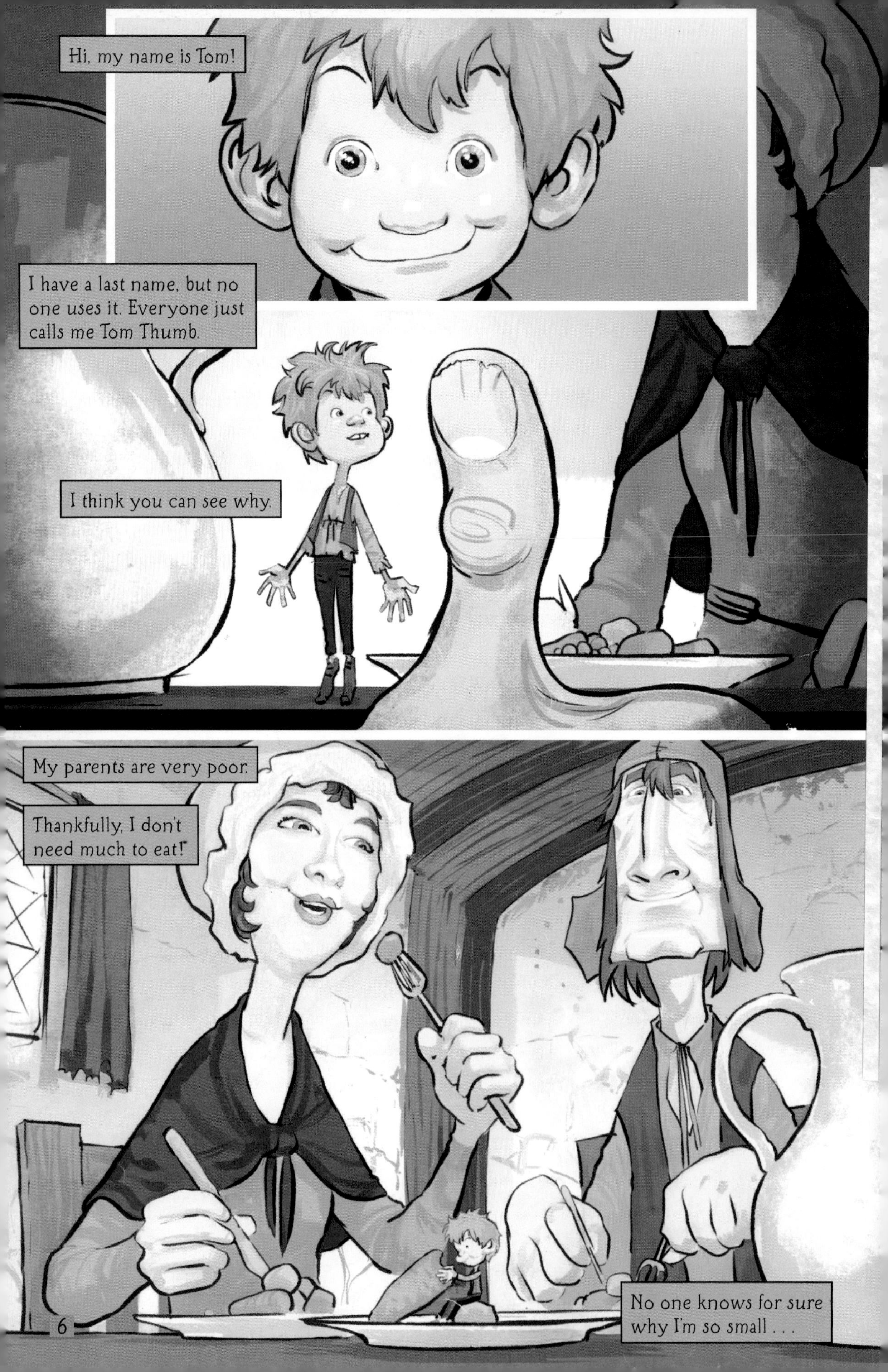
Hi, my name is Tom!
I have a last name, but no one uses it. Everyone just calls me Tom Thumb.
I think you can see why.
My parents are very poor.
Thankfully, I don't need much to eat!*
No one knows for sure why I'm so small . . .

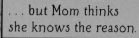

. . . but Mom thinks she knows the reason.

Your dad and I hoped to have a child for a long time.

We told each other we'd be happy to have a son "even if he were no bigger than a thumb."

And wouldn't you know it . . .

That doesn't make much sense to me. But one thing's for sure . . .

. . . Mom and Dad are glad to have me around!

So, I had a fun childhood . . .

7

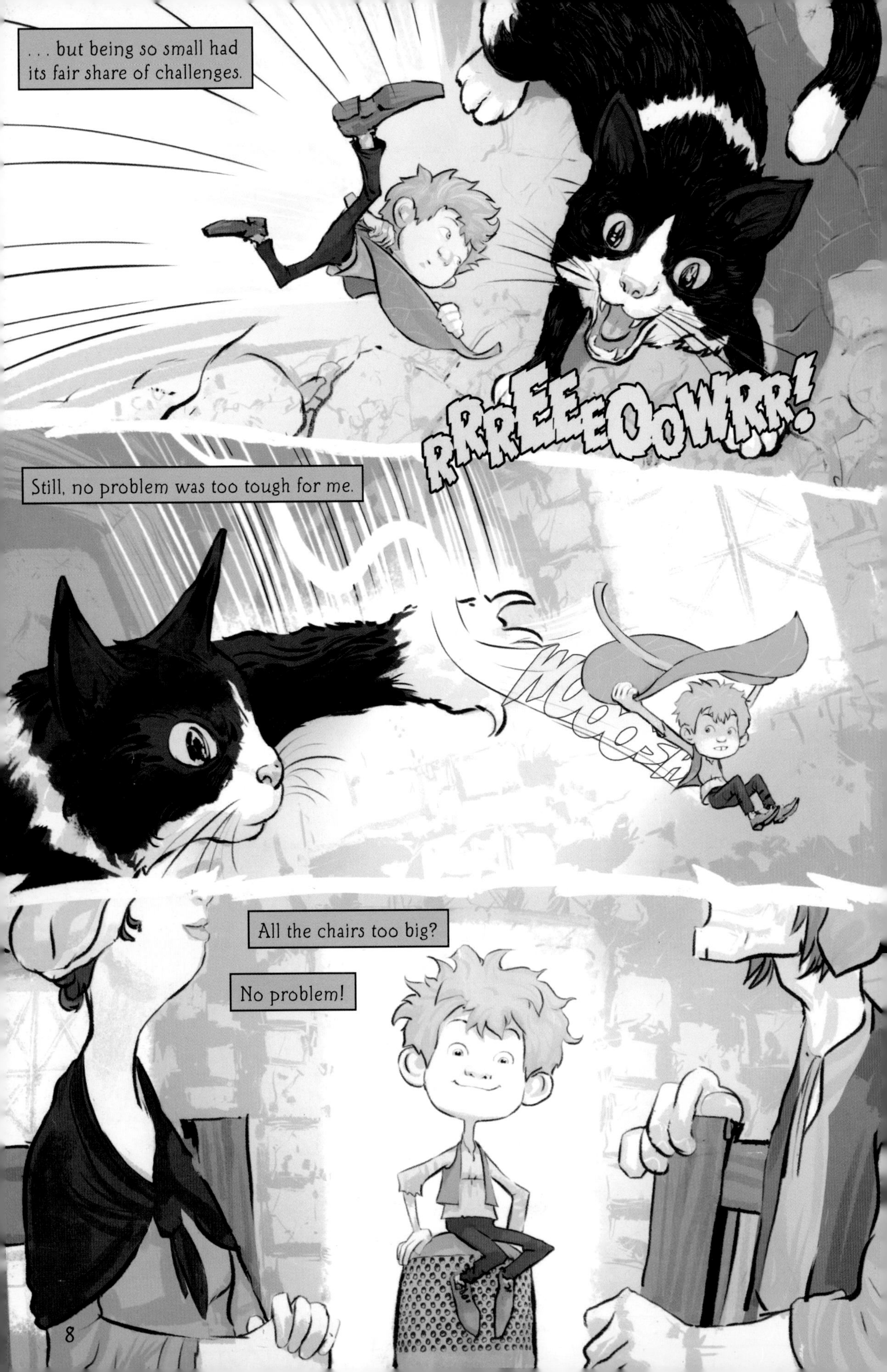
. . . but being so small had its fair share of challenges.
RRREEEOOWRR!
Still, no problem was too tough for me.
All the chairs too big?
No problem!

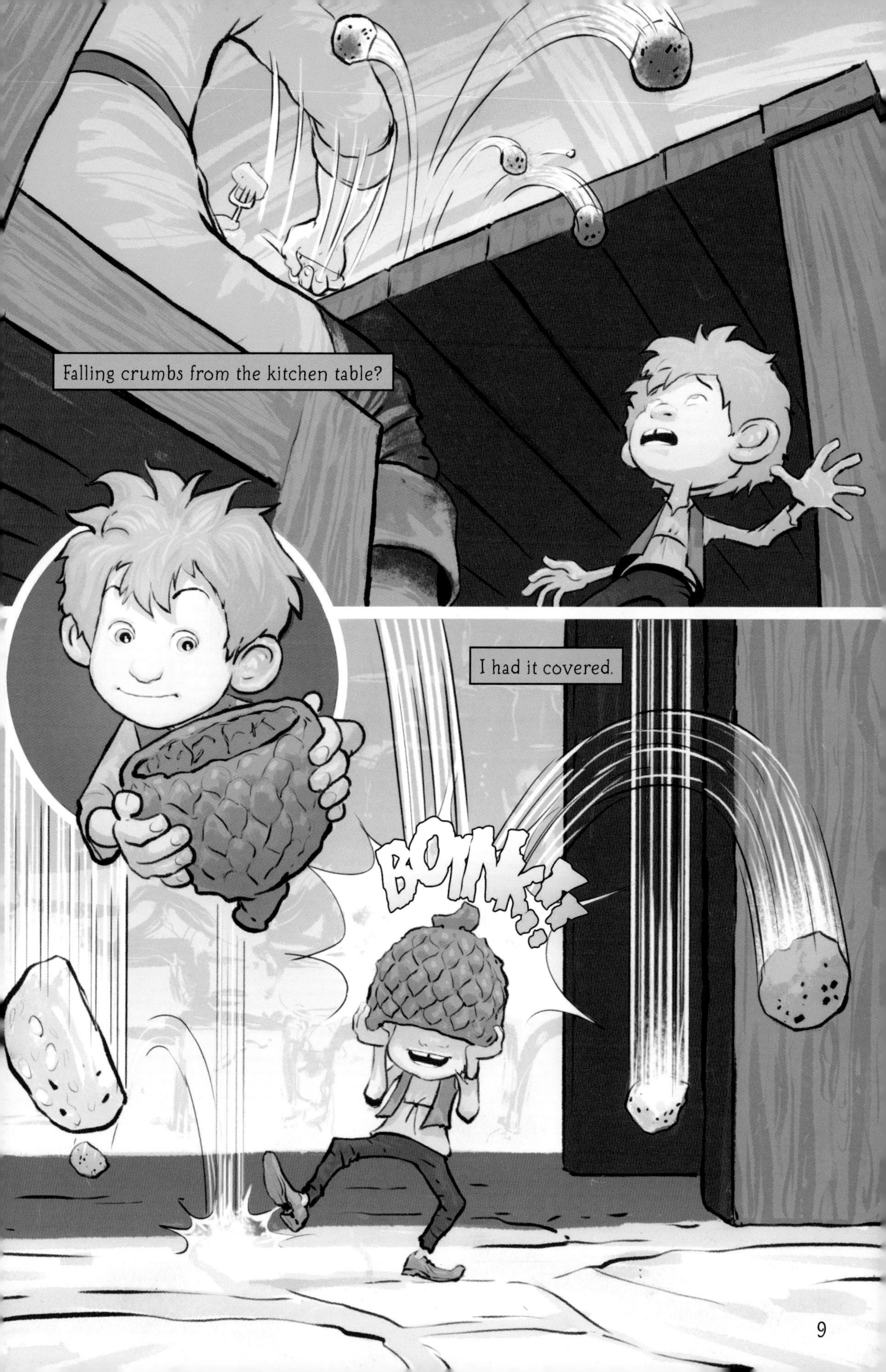
Falling crumbs from the kitchen table?
I had it covered.
BOINK!!

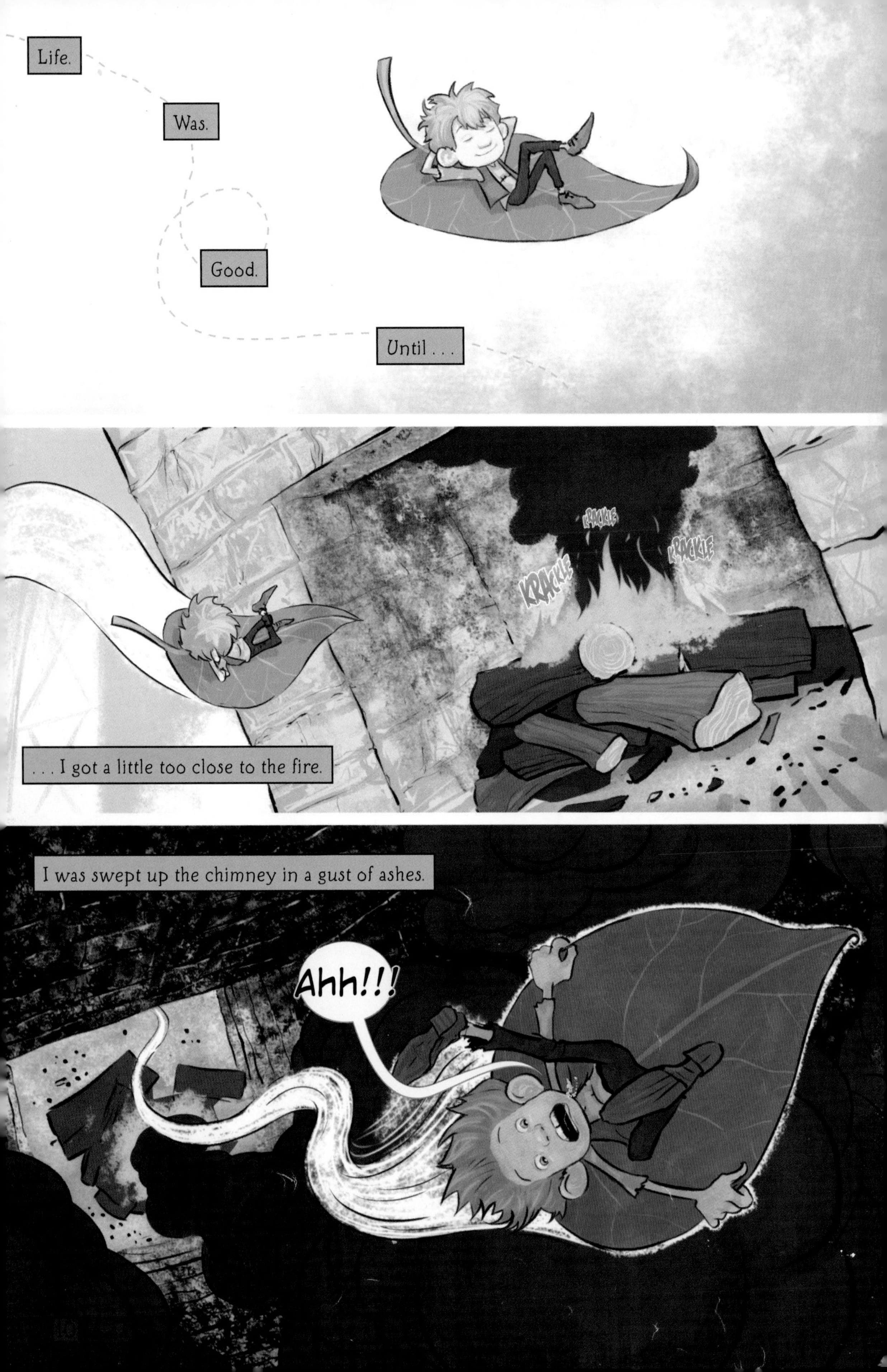
Life.
Was.
Good.
Until . . .
KRACKLE
KRACKLE
KRACKLE
. . . I got a little too close to the fire.
I was swept up the chimney in a gust of ashes.
Ahh!!!

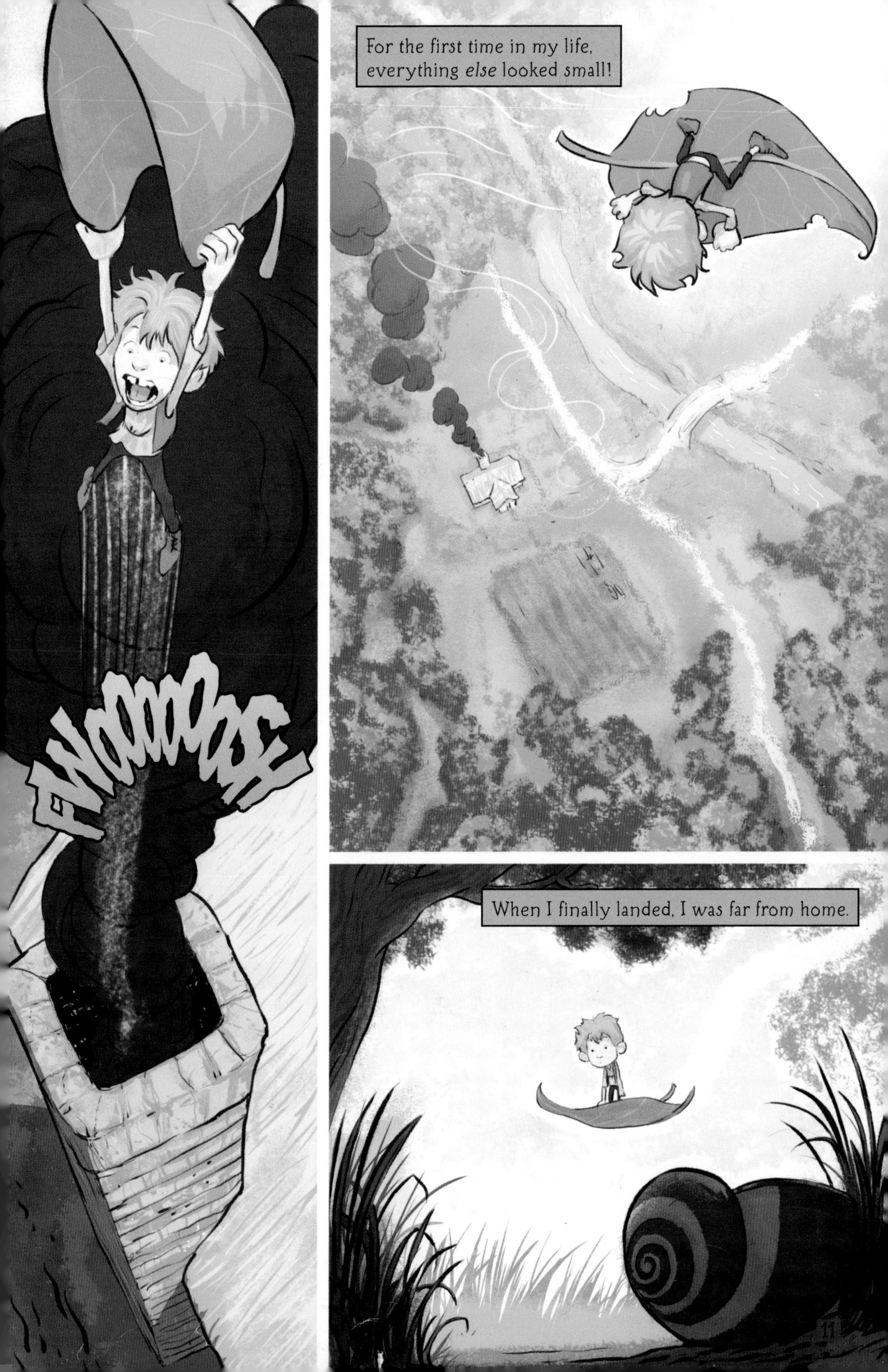
FWOOOOSH!
For the first time in my life, everything *else* looked small!
When I finally landed, I was far from home.

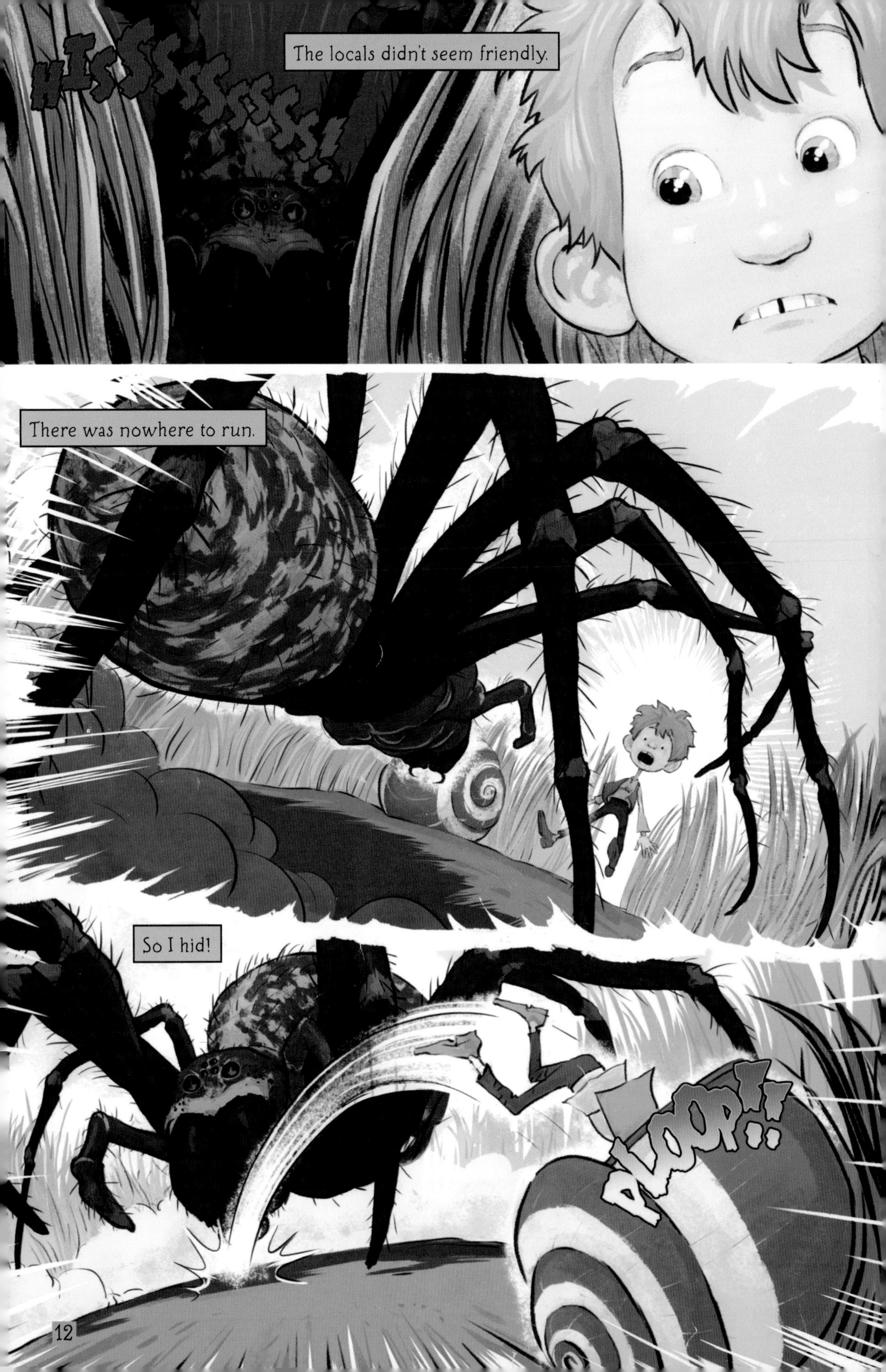
HISSSSSSSSSS!
The locals didn't seem friendly.
There was nowhere to run.
So I hid!
PLOOP!!!

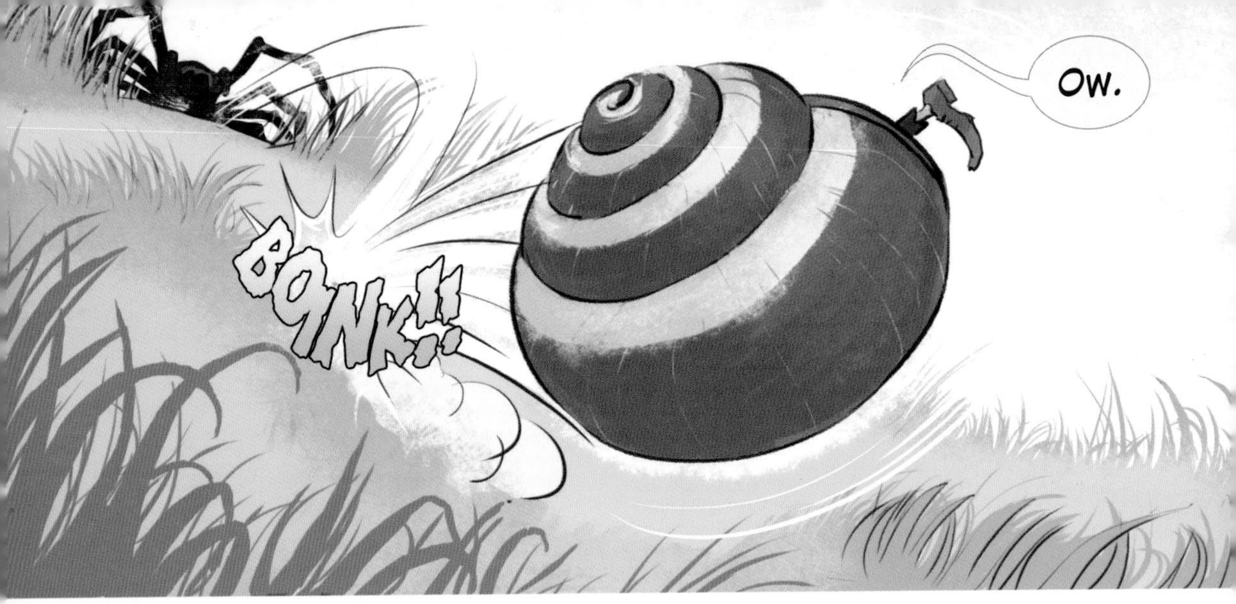
BOINK!!
OW.

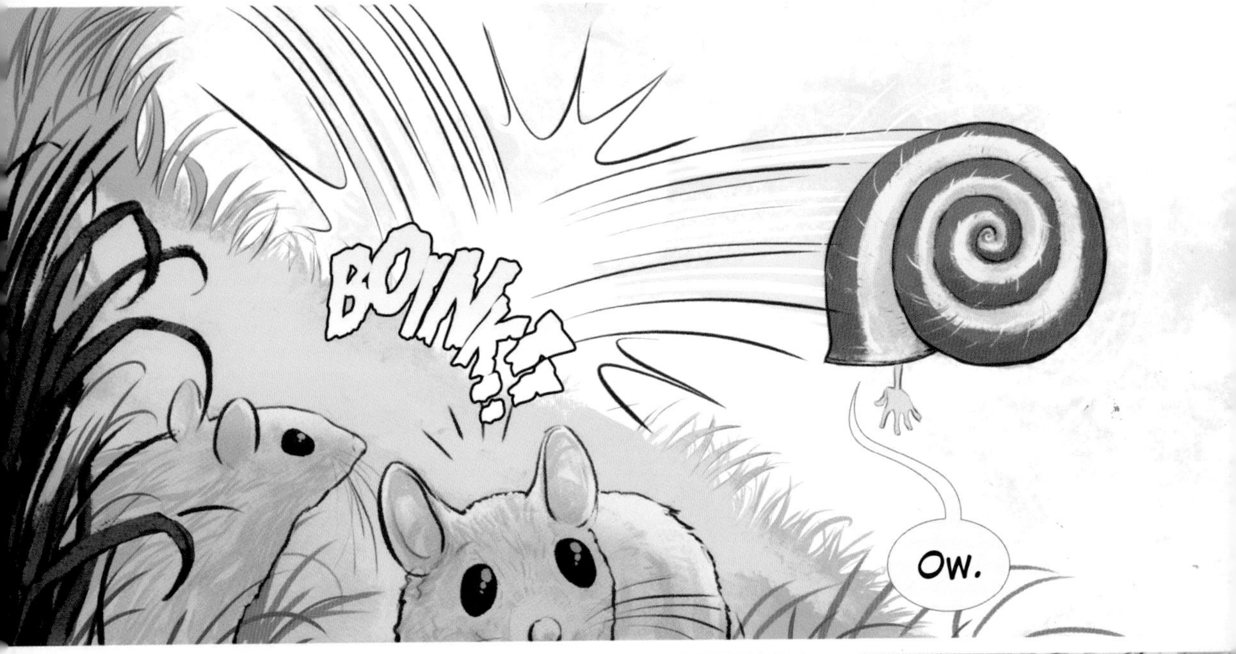
BOINK!!
OW.

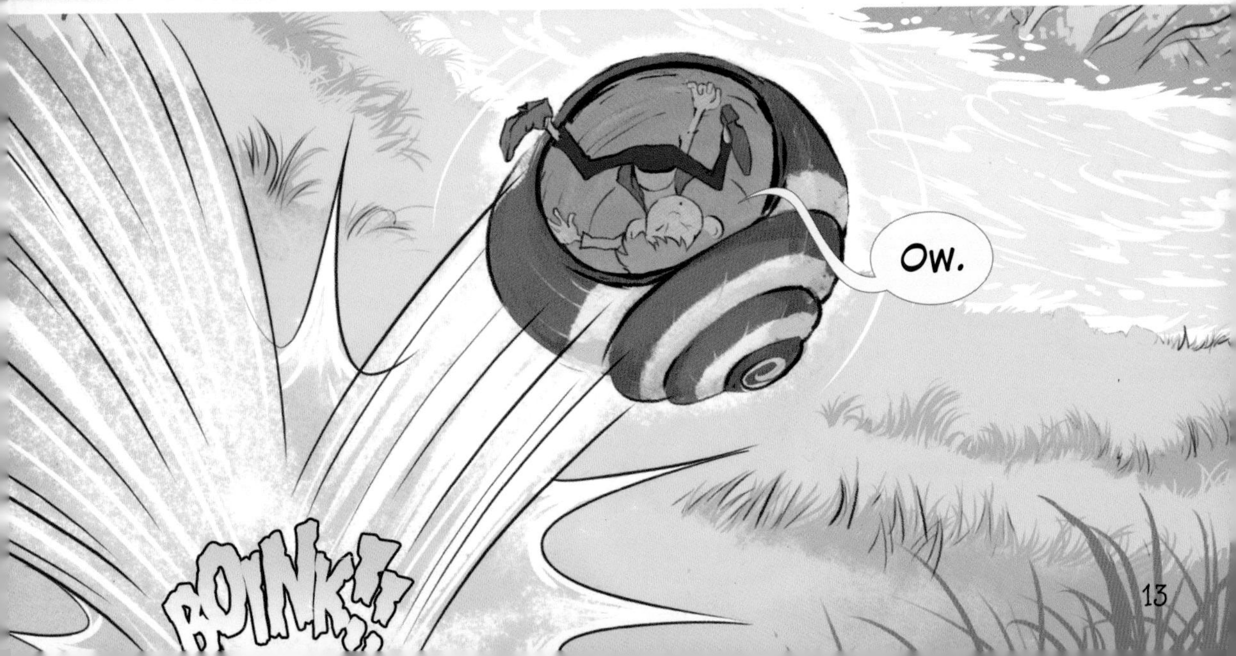
OW.
BOINK!!

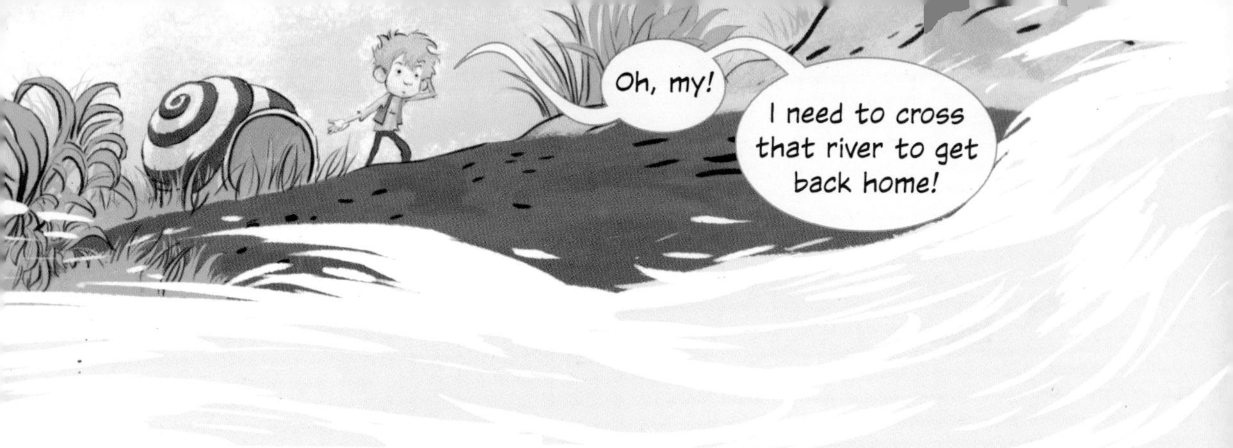
Oh, my!
I need to cross that river to get back home!

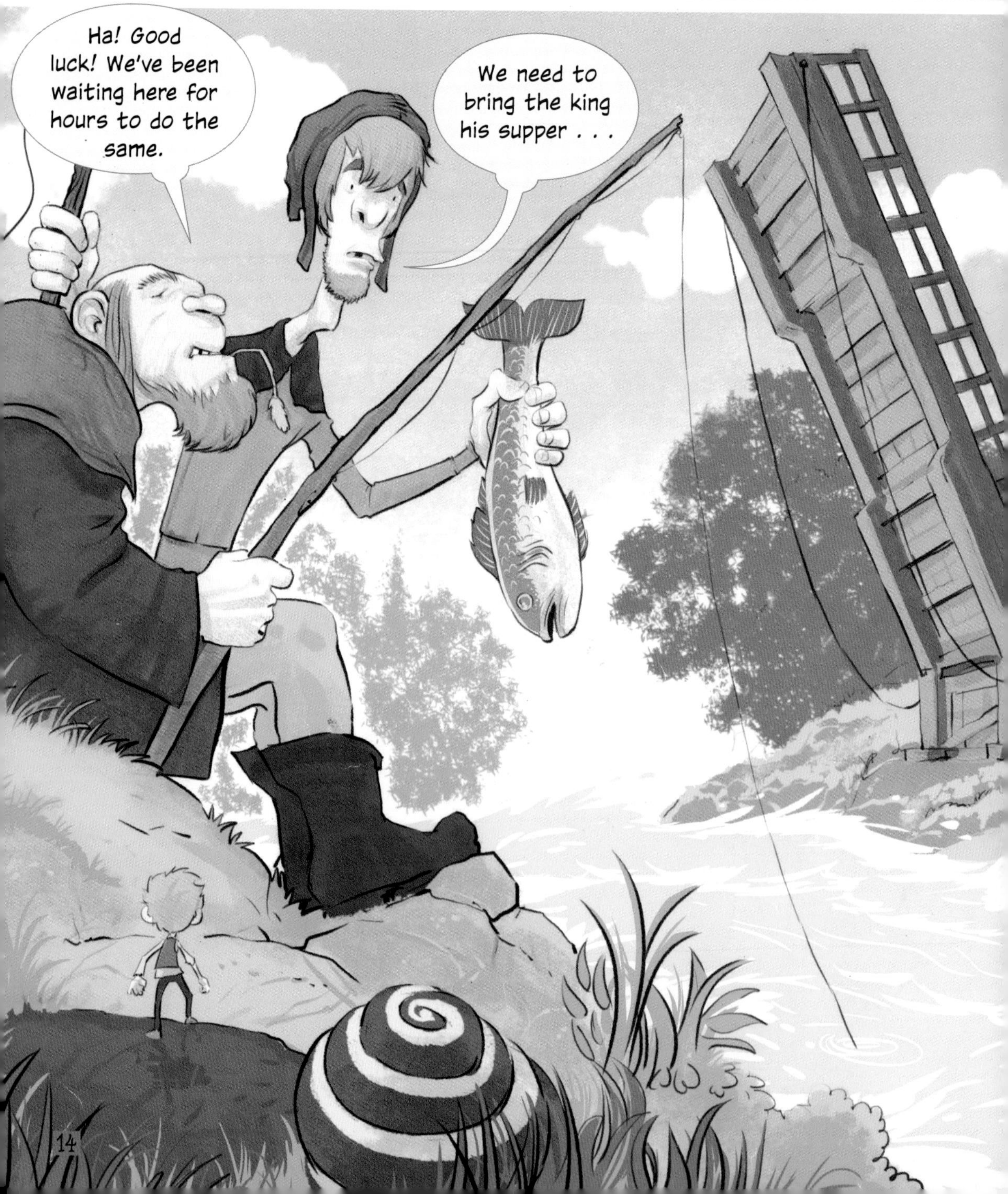
Ha! Good luck! We've been waiting here for hours to do the same.
We need to bring the king his supper . . .

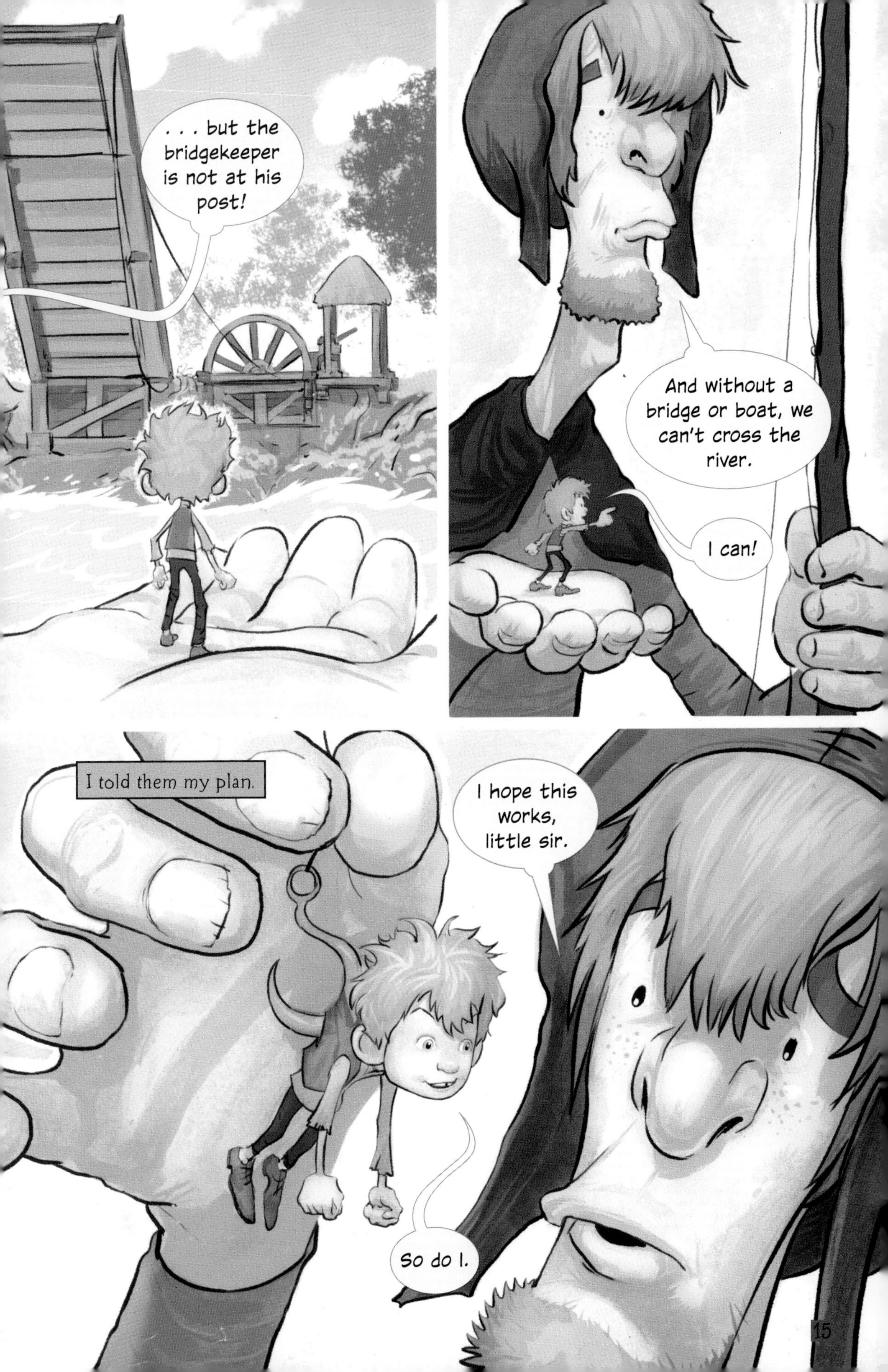

. . . but the bridgekeeper is not at his post!
And without a bridge or boat, we can't cross the river.
I can!
I told them my plan.
I hope this works, little sir.
So do I.

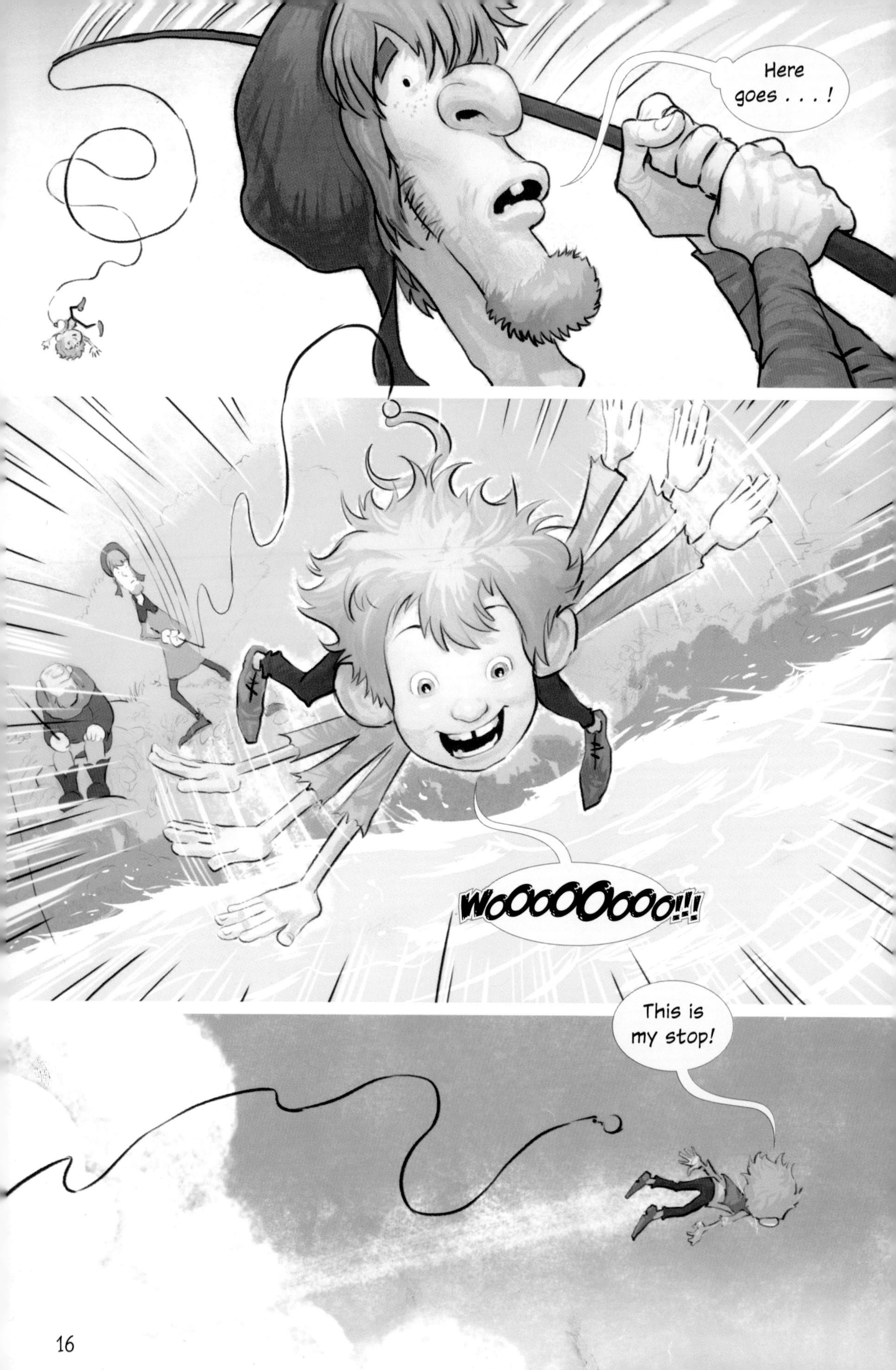
Here goes . . . !
WOOOOOOOO!!!
This is my stop!

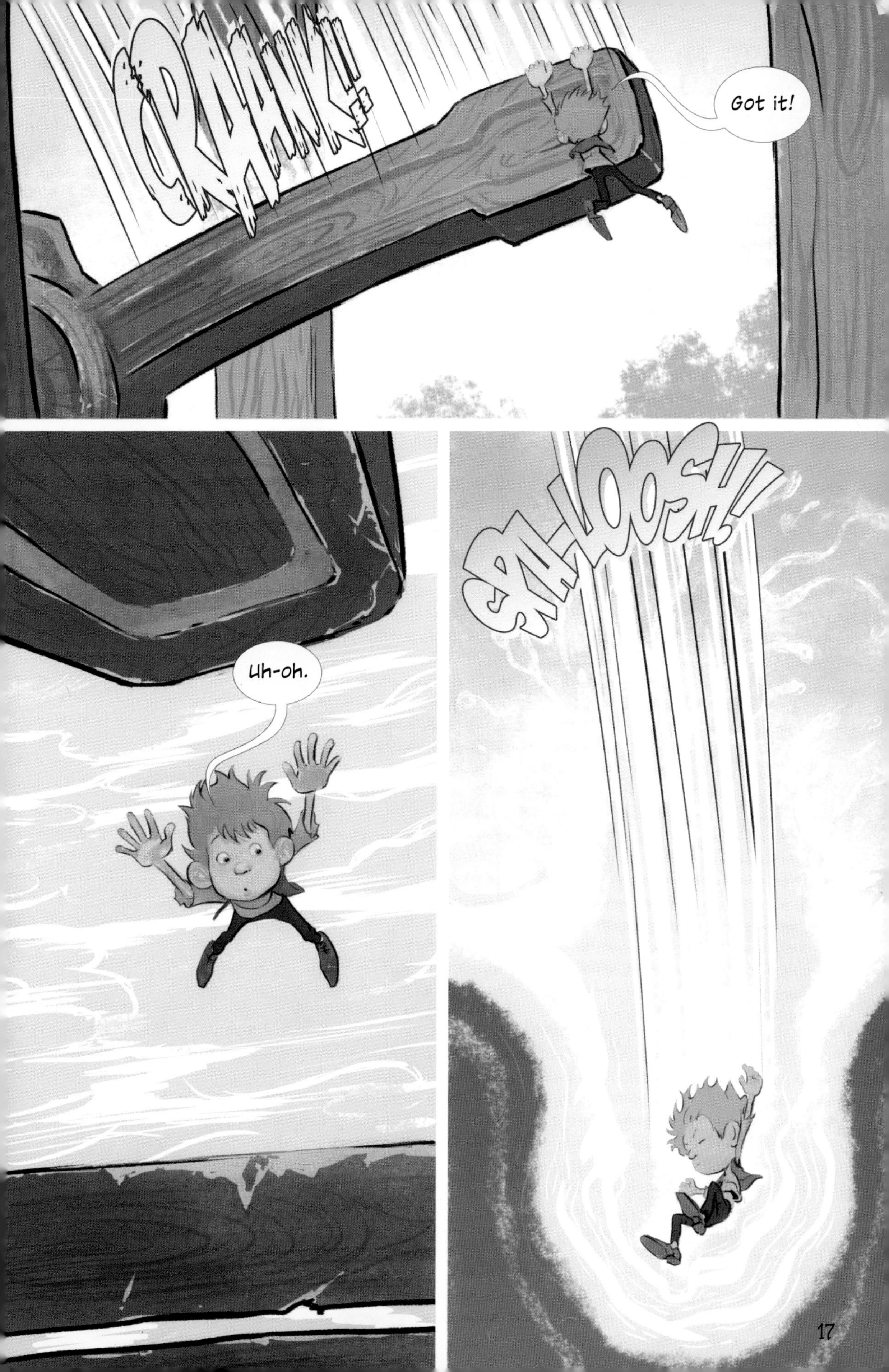
CRANK!!
Got it!
Uh-oh.
SPA-LOOSH!!

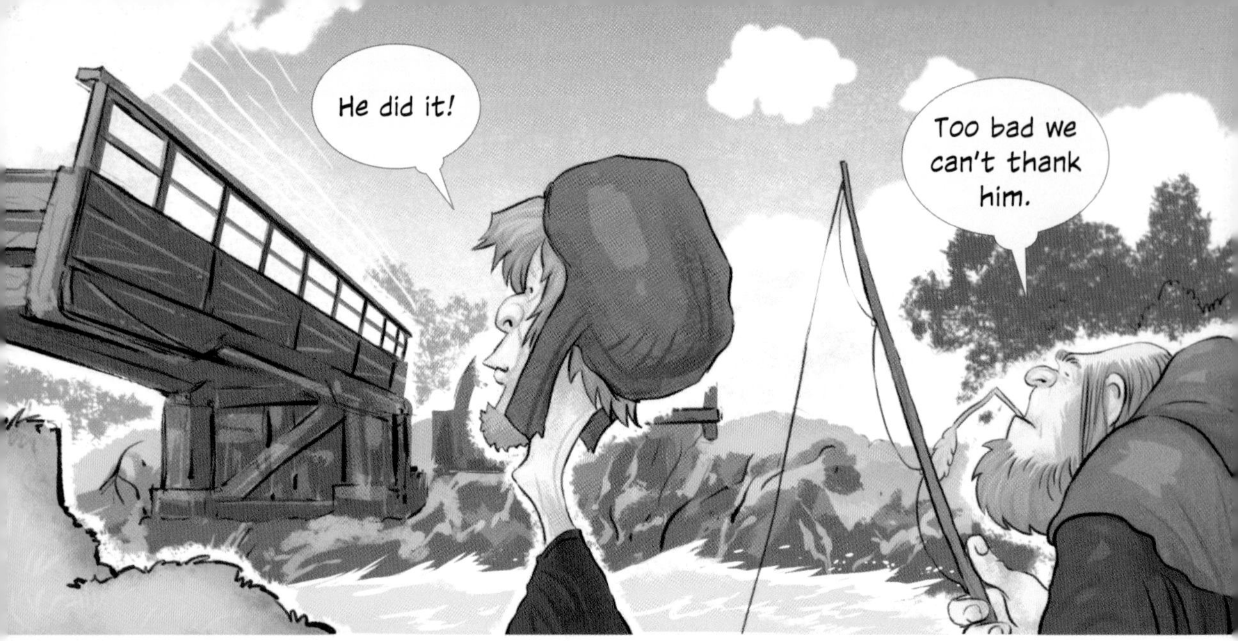
He did it!
Too bad we can't thank him.

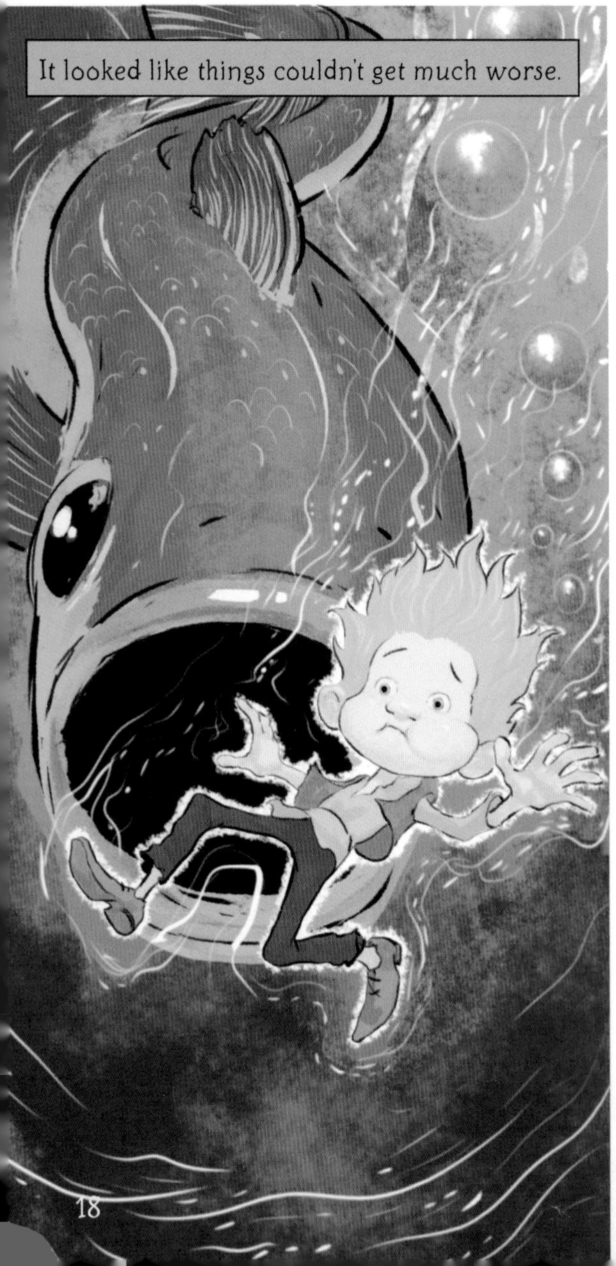
It looked like things couldn't get much worse.

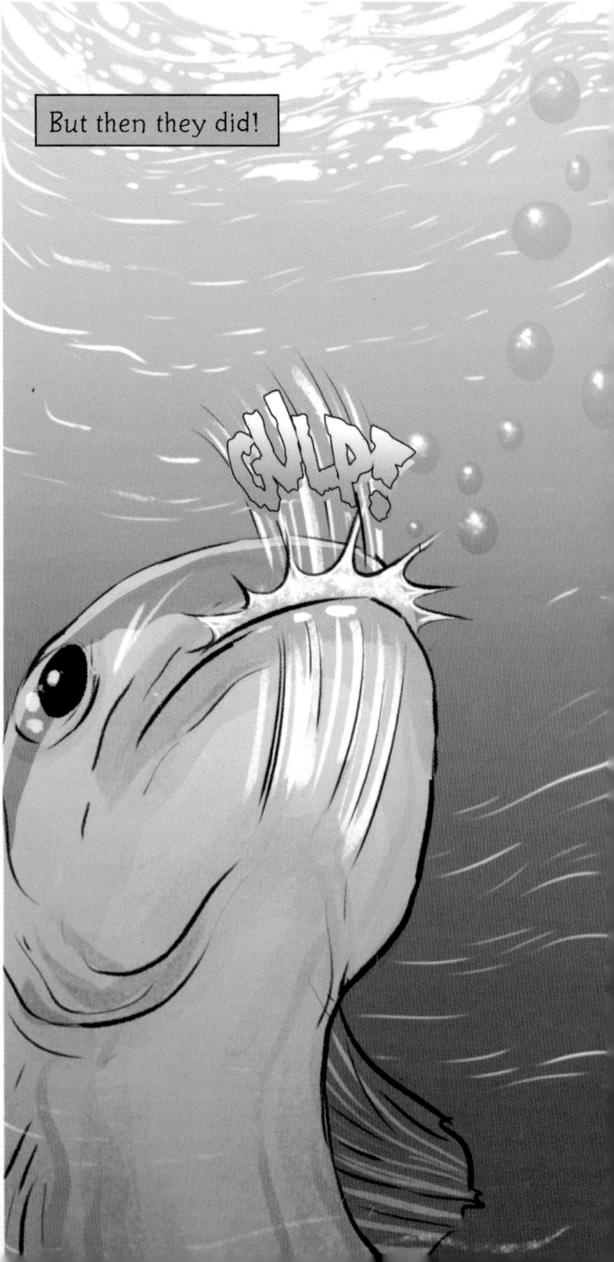
But then they did!
GULP!

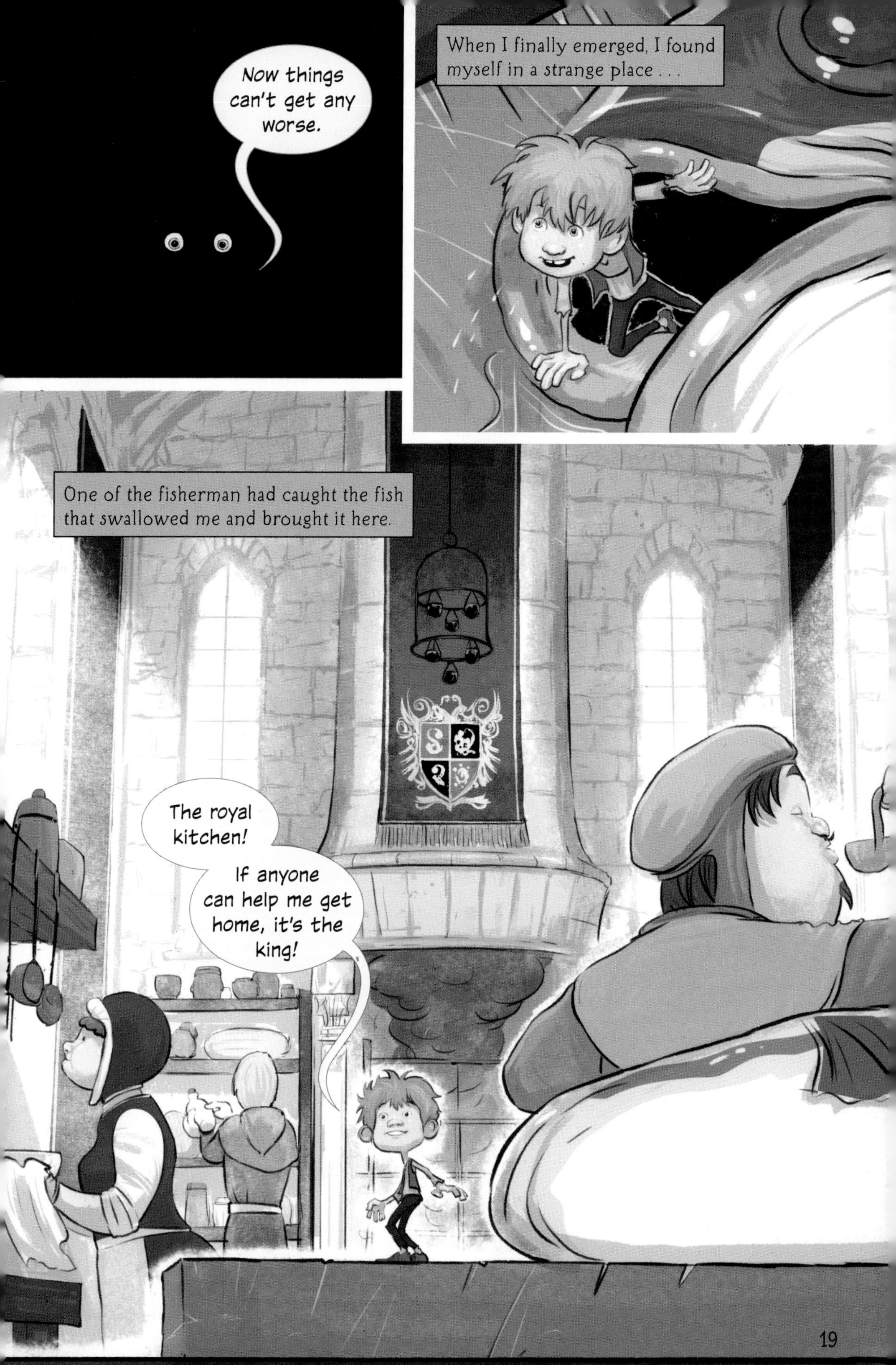
Now things can't get any worse.
When I finally emerged, I found myself in a strange place . . .
One of the fisherman had caught the fish that swallowed me and brought it here.
The royal kitchen!
If anyone can help me get home, it's the king!

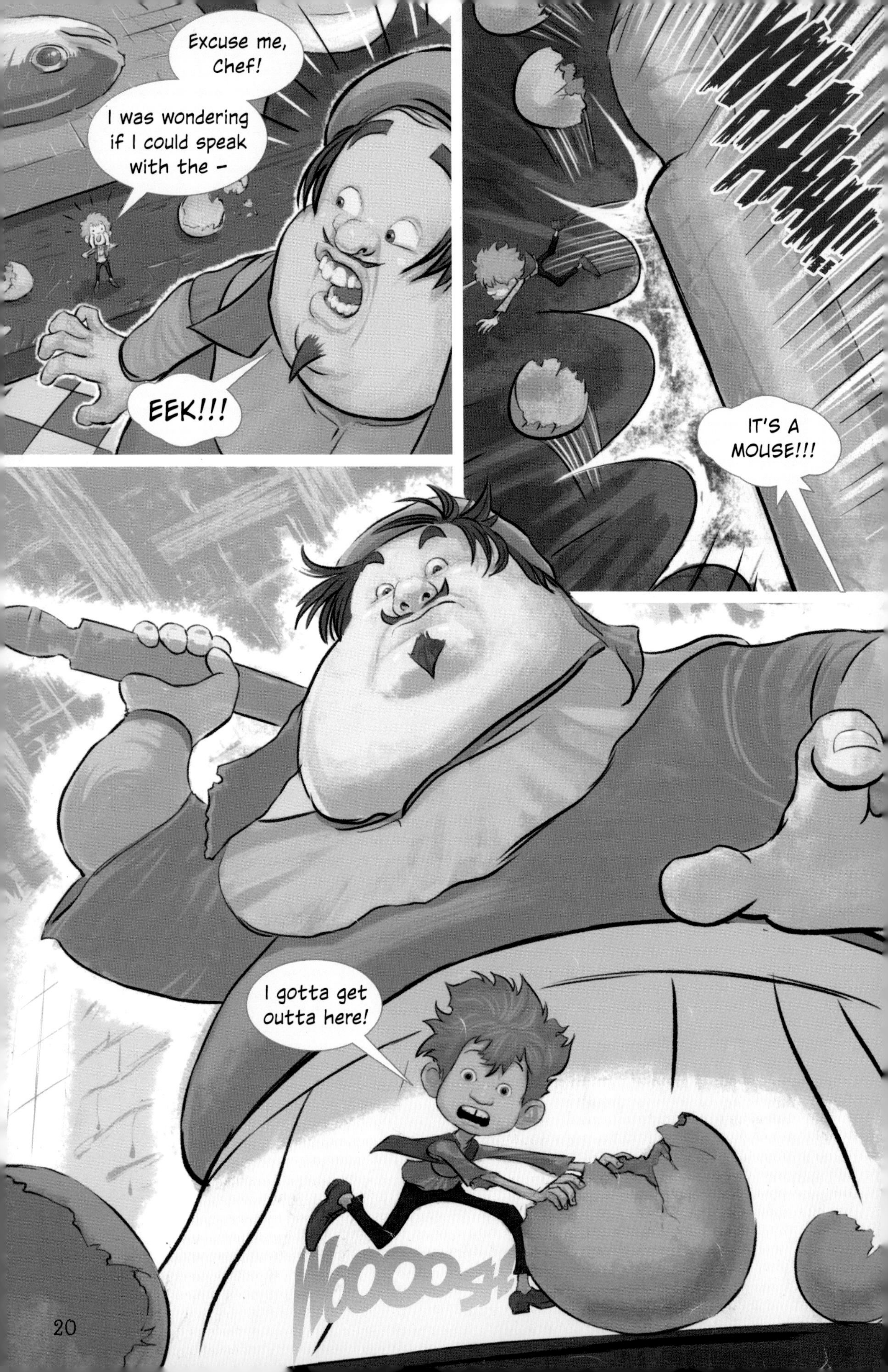

Excuse me, Chef!
I was wondering if I could speak with the –
EEK!!!
WHAM!
IT'S A MOUSE!!!
I gotta get outta here!
WOOOSH

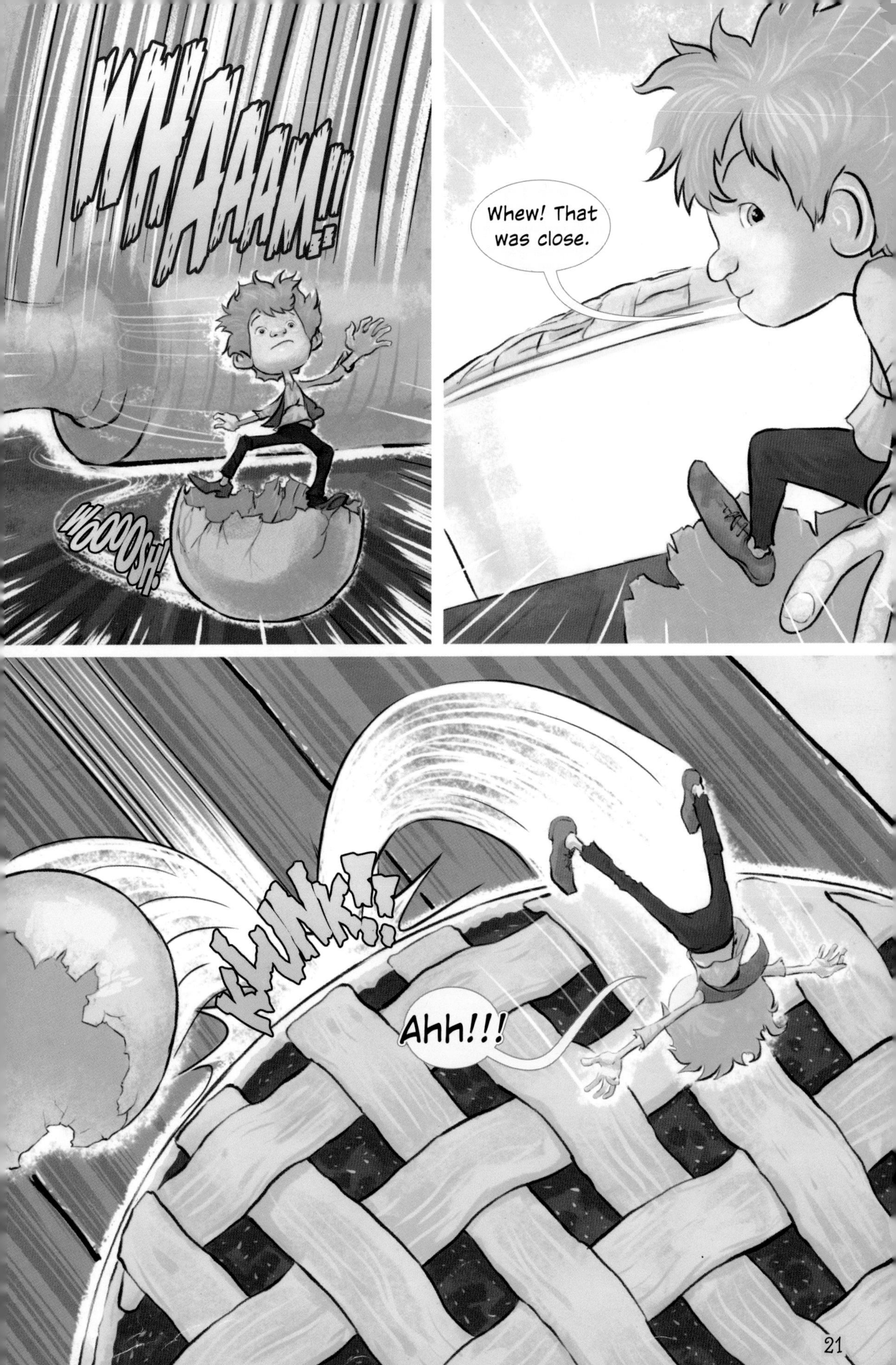
WHAAAM!!
WOOOOSH!
Whew! That was close.
KLUNK!!!
Ahh!!!

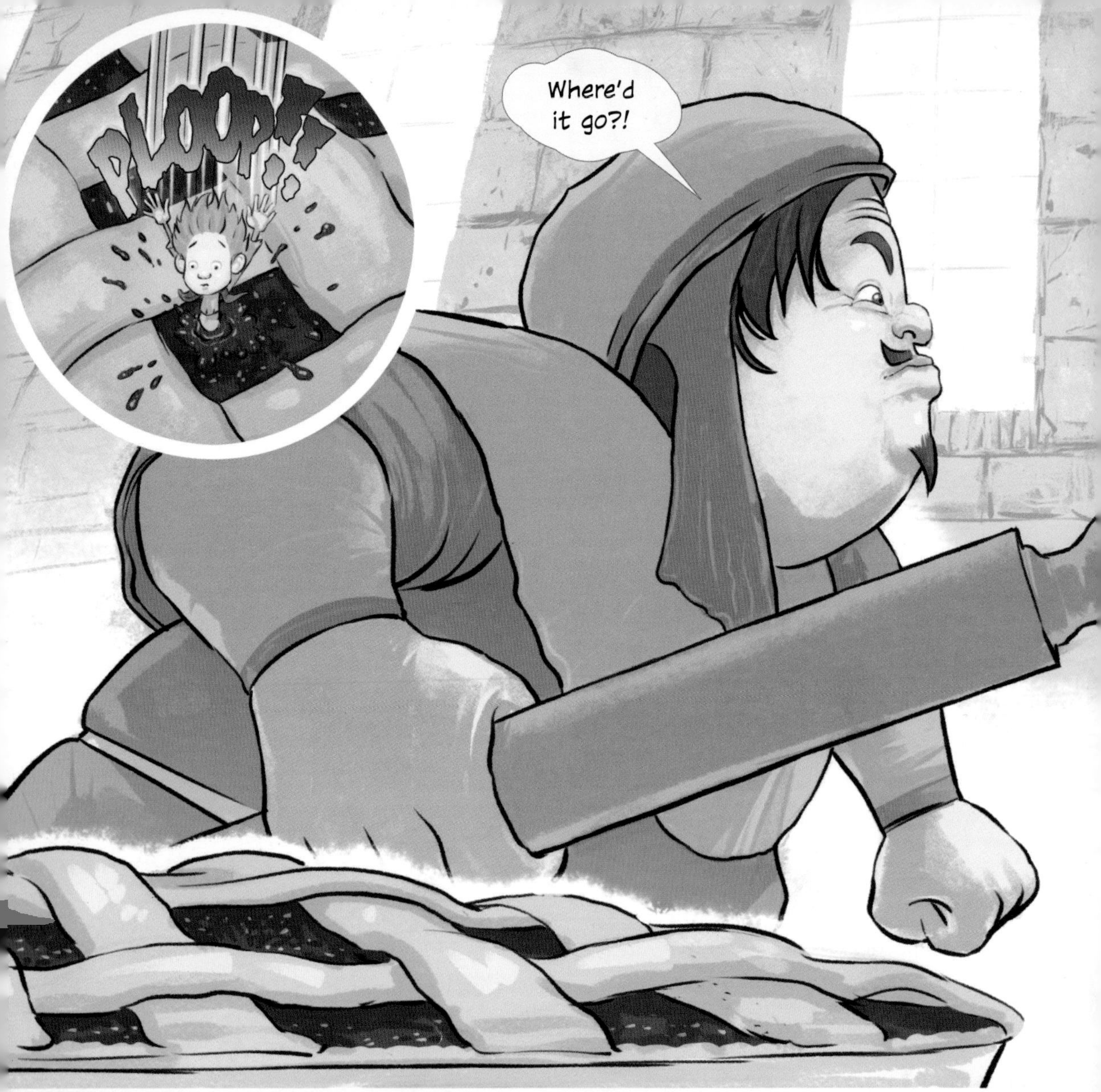
PLOOP!!
Where'd it go?!

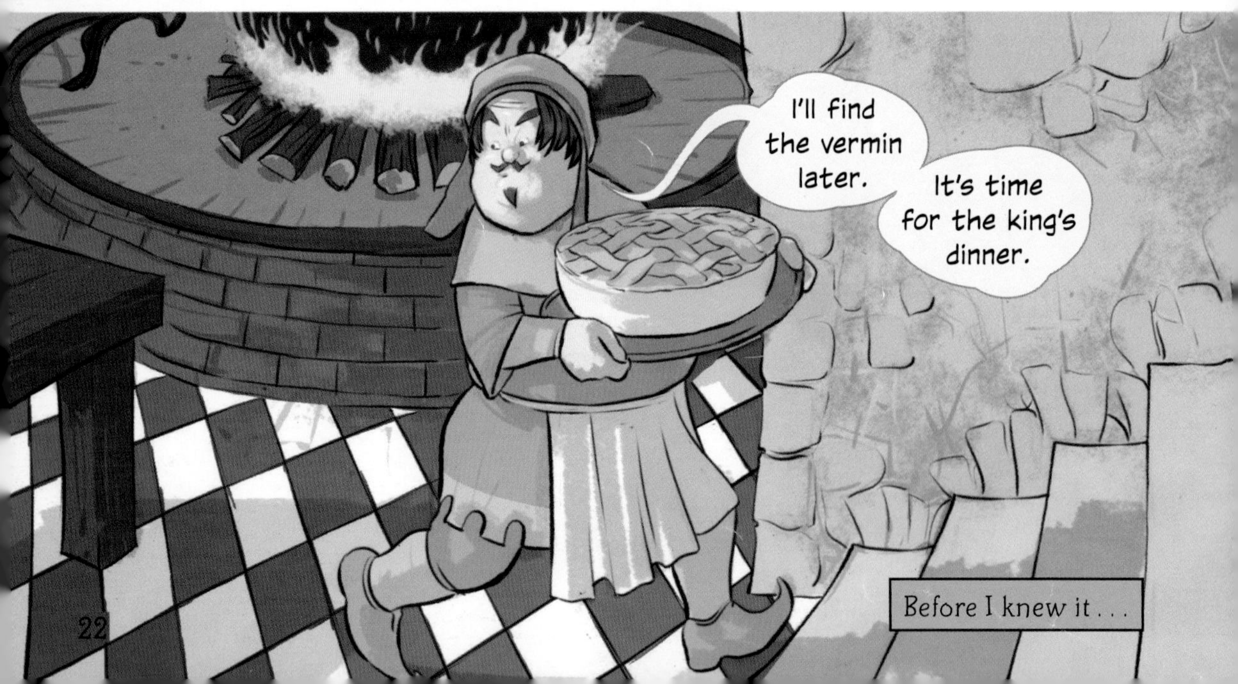
I'll find the vermin later.
It's time for the king's dinner.
Before I knew it . . .

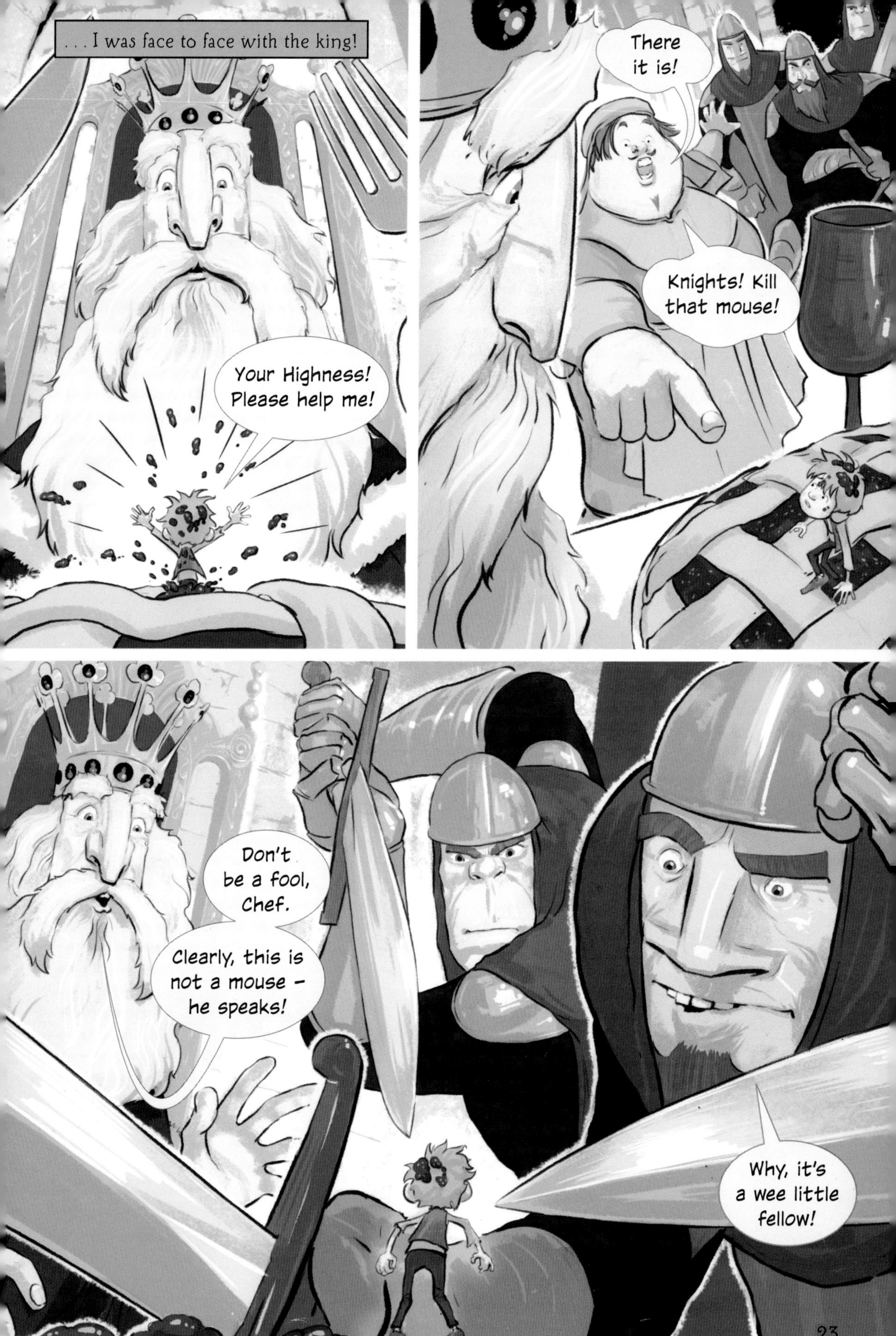
. . . I was face to face with the king!
Your Highness! Please help me!
There it is!
Knights! Kill that mouse!
Don't be a fool, Chef.
Clearly, this is not a mouse – he speaks!
Why, it's a wee little fellow!

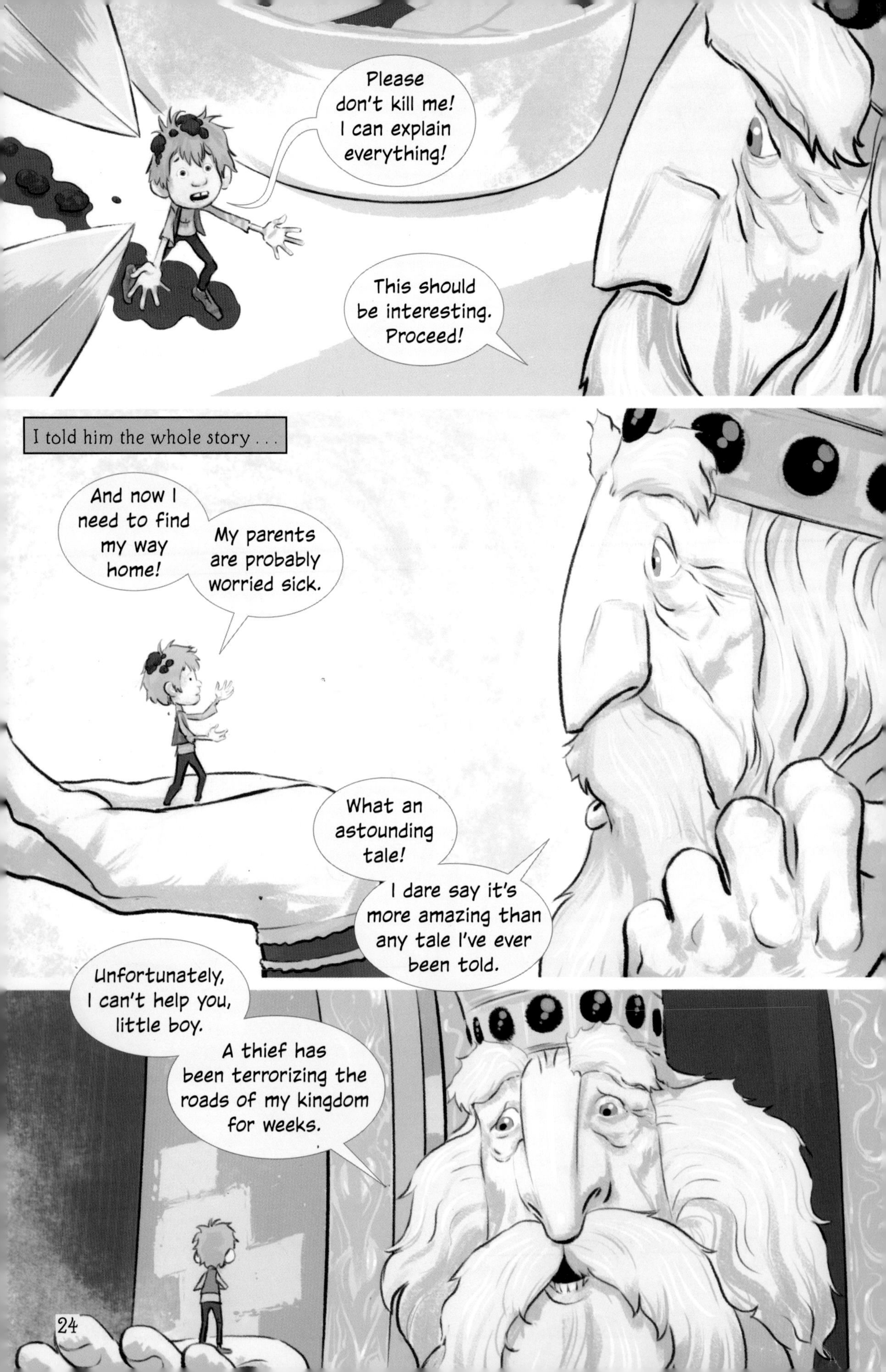
Please don't kill me! I can explain everything!
This should be interesting. Proceed!
I told him the whole story . . .
And now I need to find my way home!
My parents are probably worried sick.
What an astounding tale!
I dare say it's more amazing than any tale I've ever been told.
Unfortunately, I can't help you, little boy.
A thief has been terrorizing the roads of my kingdom for weeks.

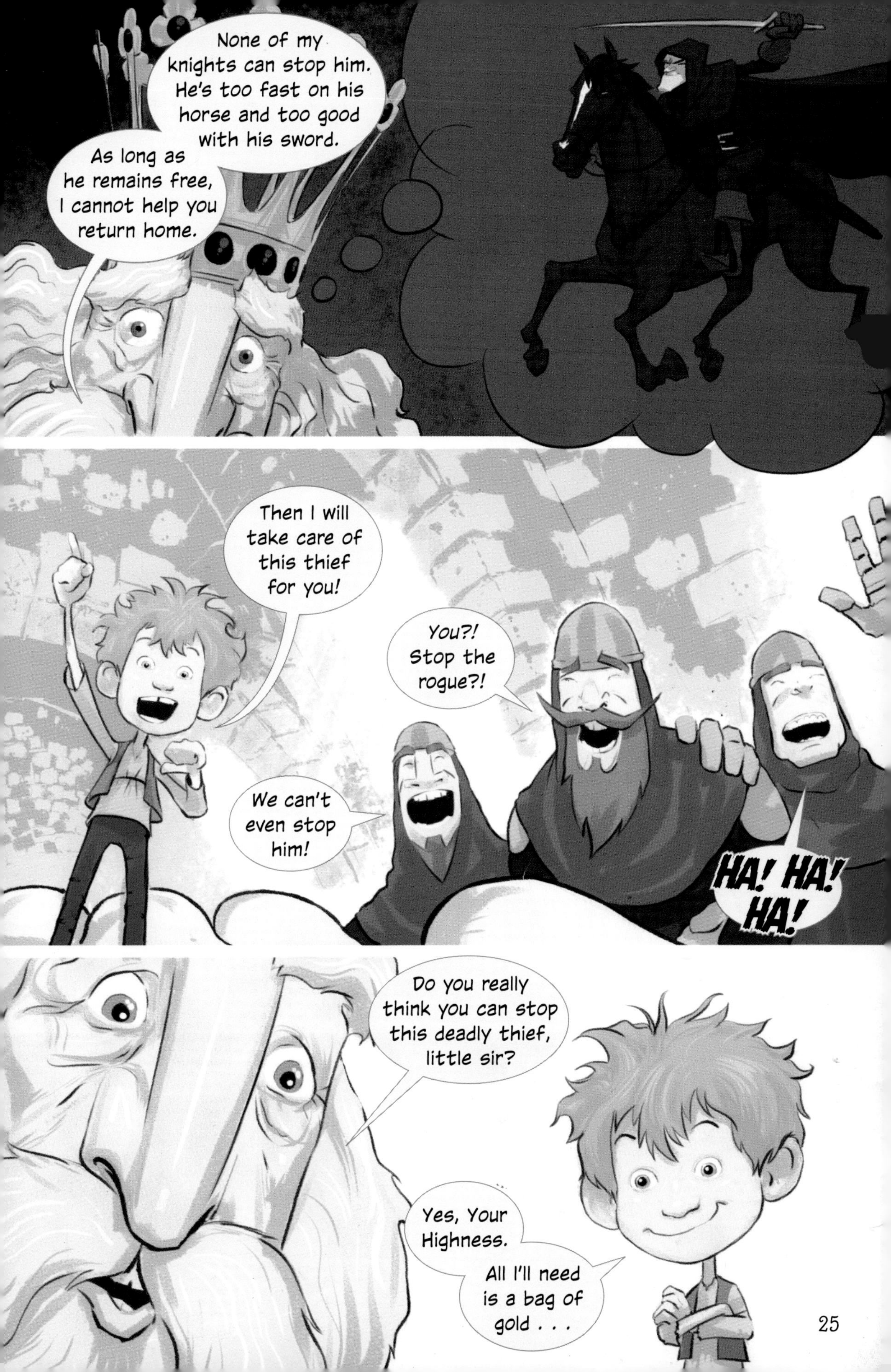
None of my knights can stop him. He's too fast on his horse and too good with his sword.
As long as he remains free, I cannot help you return home.
Then I will take care of this thief for you!
You?! Stop the rogue?!
We can't even stop him!
HA! HA! HA!
Do you really think you can stop this deadly thief, little sir?
Yes, Your Highness.
All I'll need is a bag of gold . . .

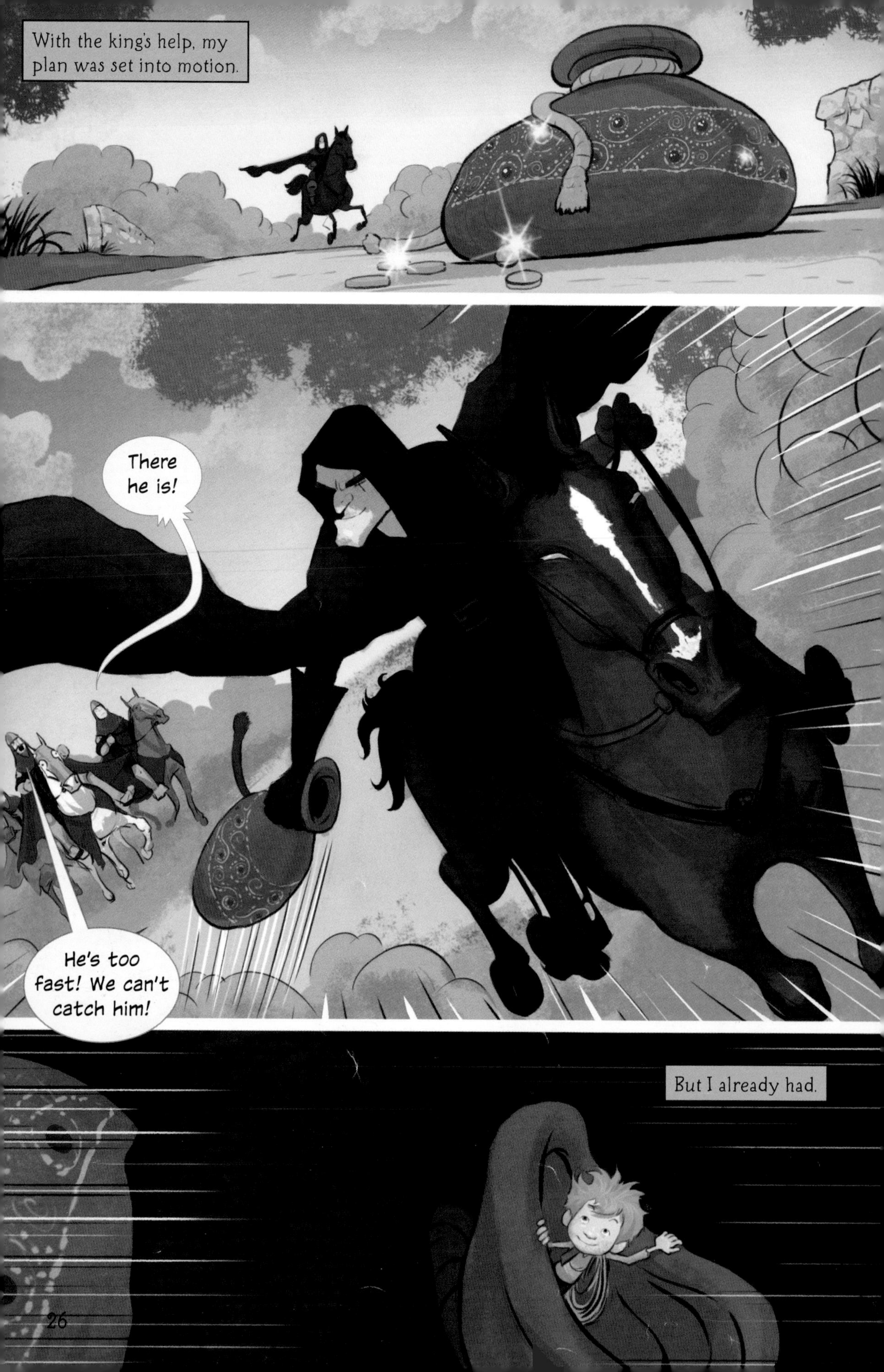
With the king's help, my plan was set into motion.
There he is!
He's too fast! We can't catch him!
But I already had.

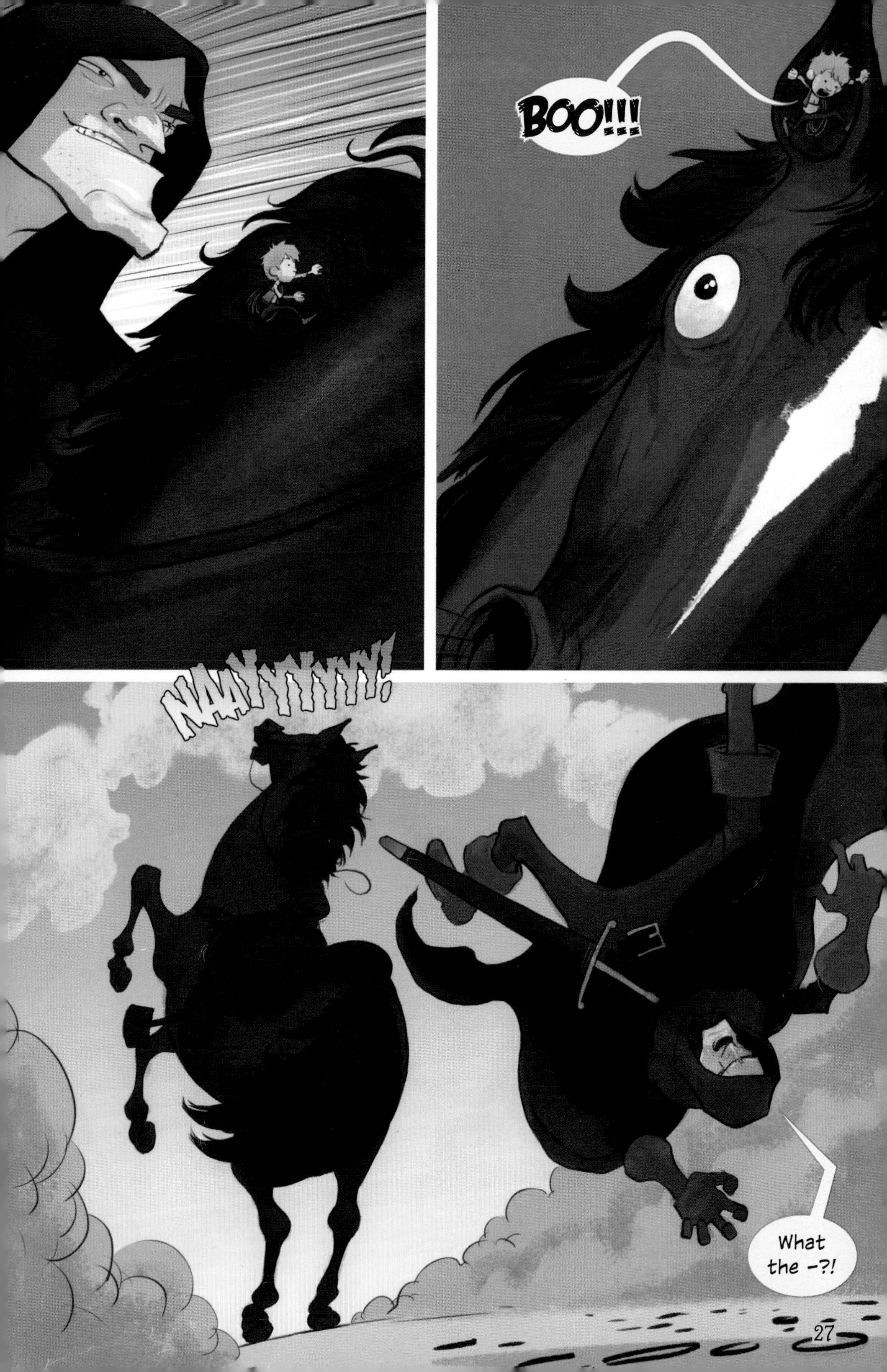
BOO!!!
NAAYYYYYY!
What the -?!

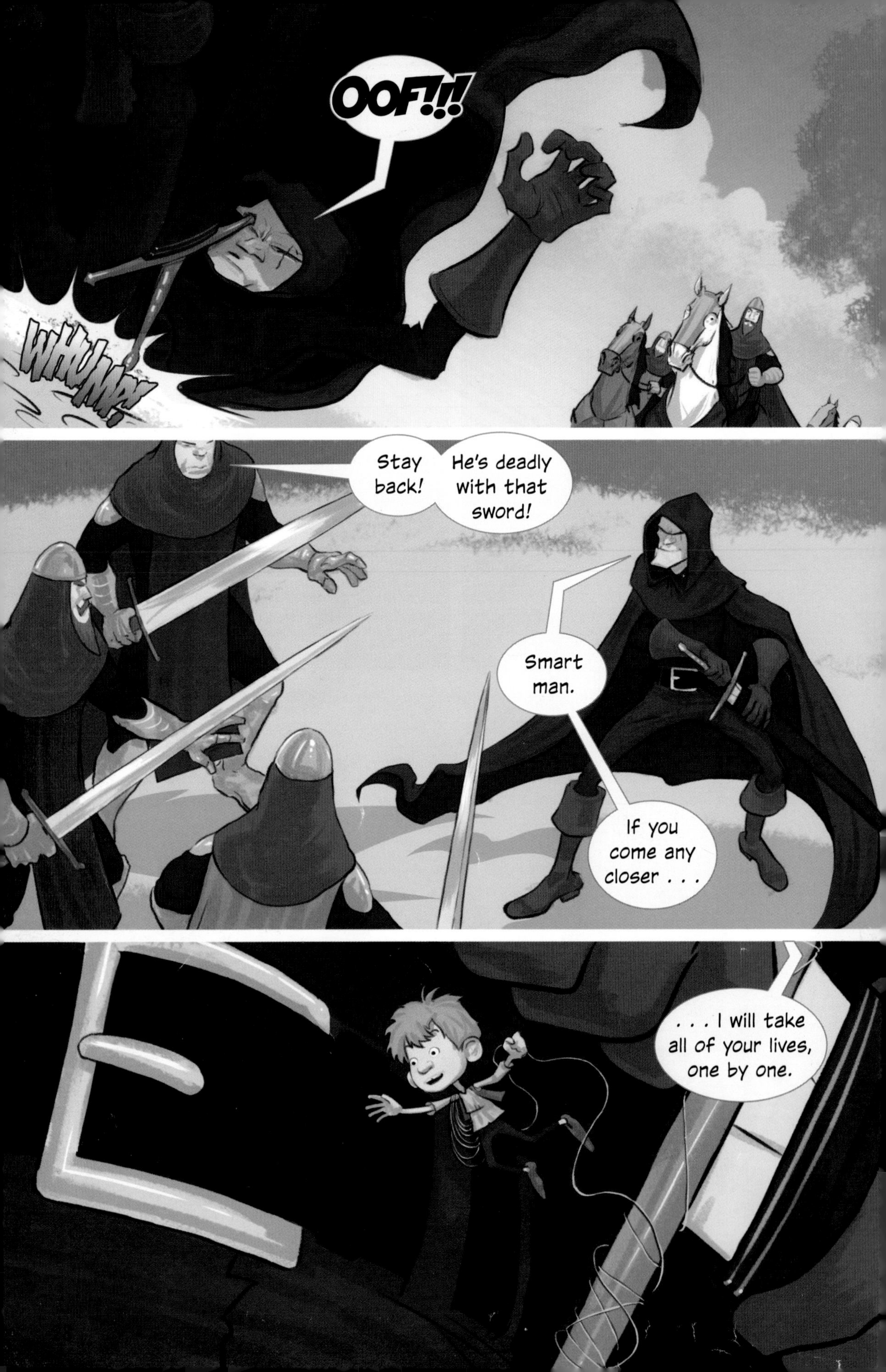
OOF!!!
WHUMP!
Stay back!
He's deadly with that sword!
Smart man.
If you come any closer . . .
. . . I will take all of your lives, one by one.

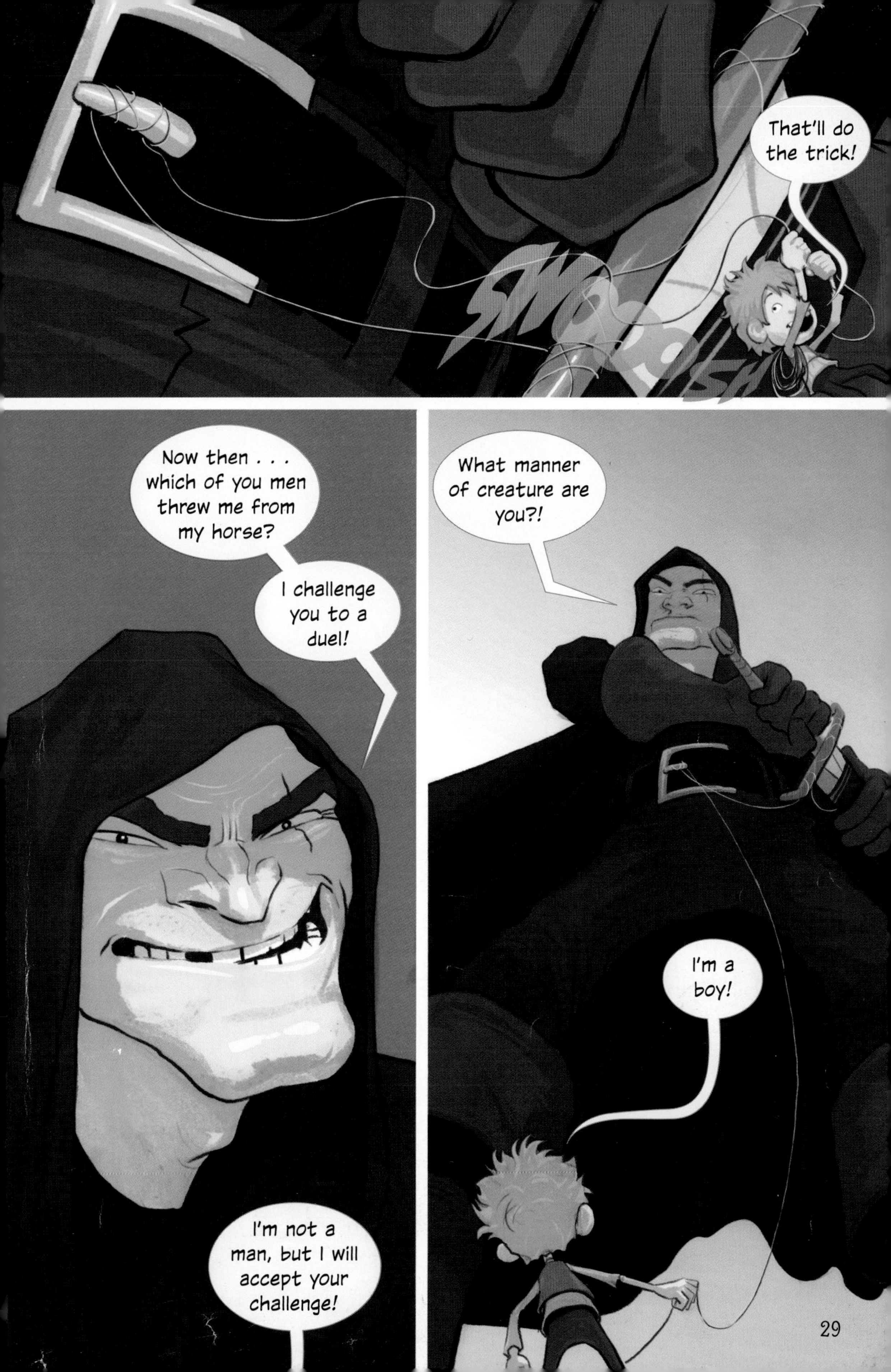
That'll do the trick!
SWOOSH
Now then . . . which of you men threw me from my horse?
I challenge you to a duel!
I'm not a man, but I will accept your challenge!
What manner of creature are you?!
I'm a boy!

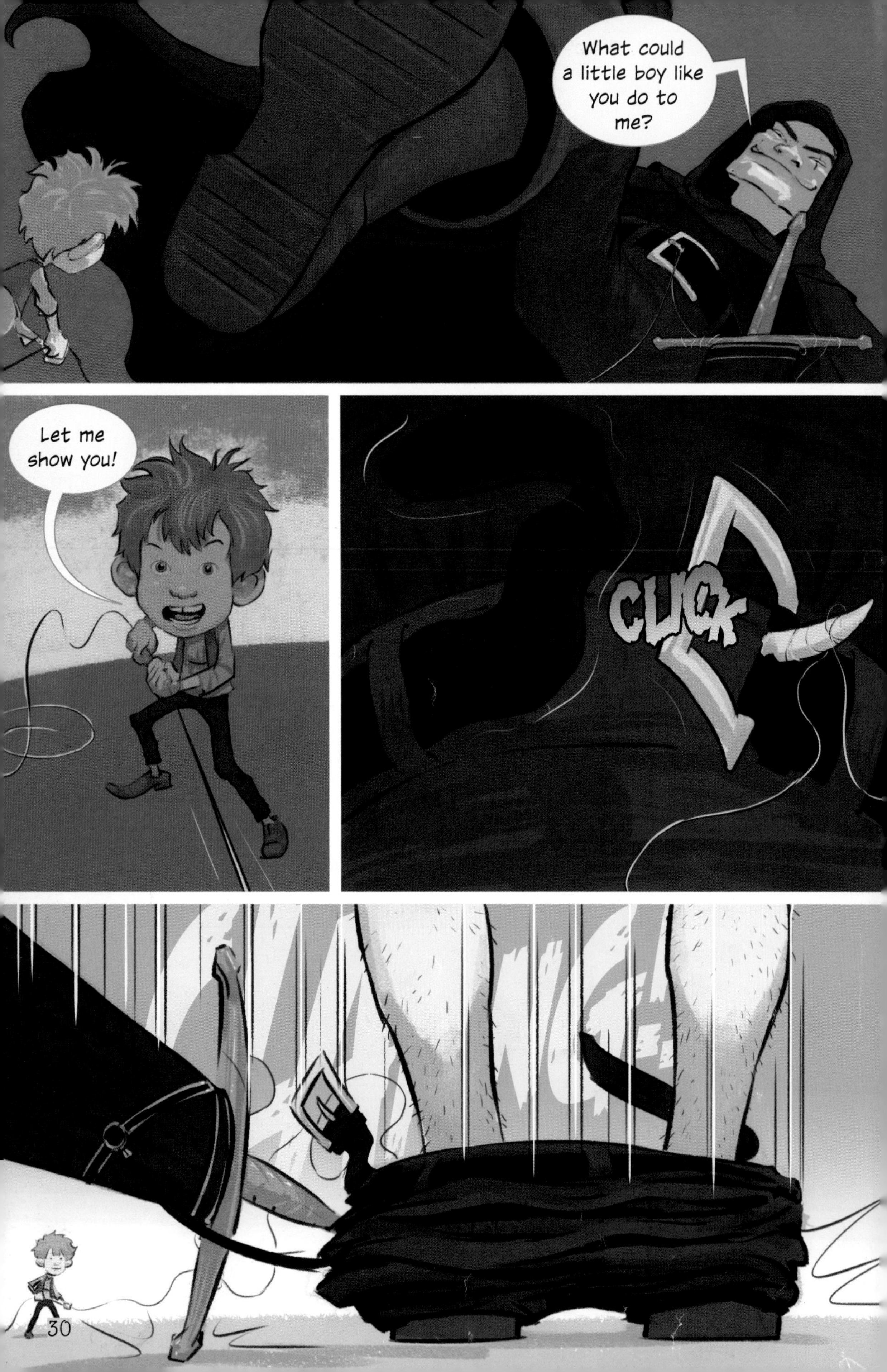
What could a little boy like you do to me?
Let me show you!
CLICK

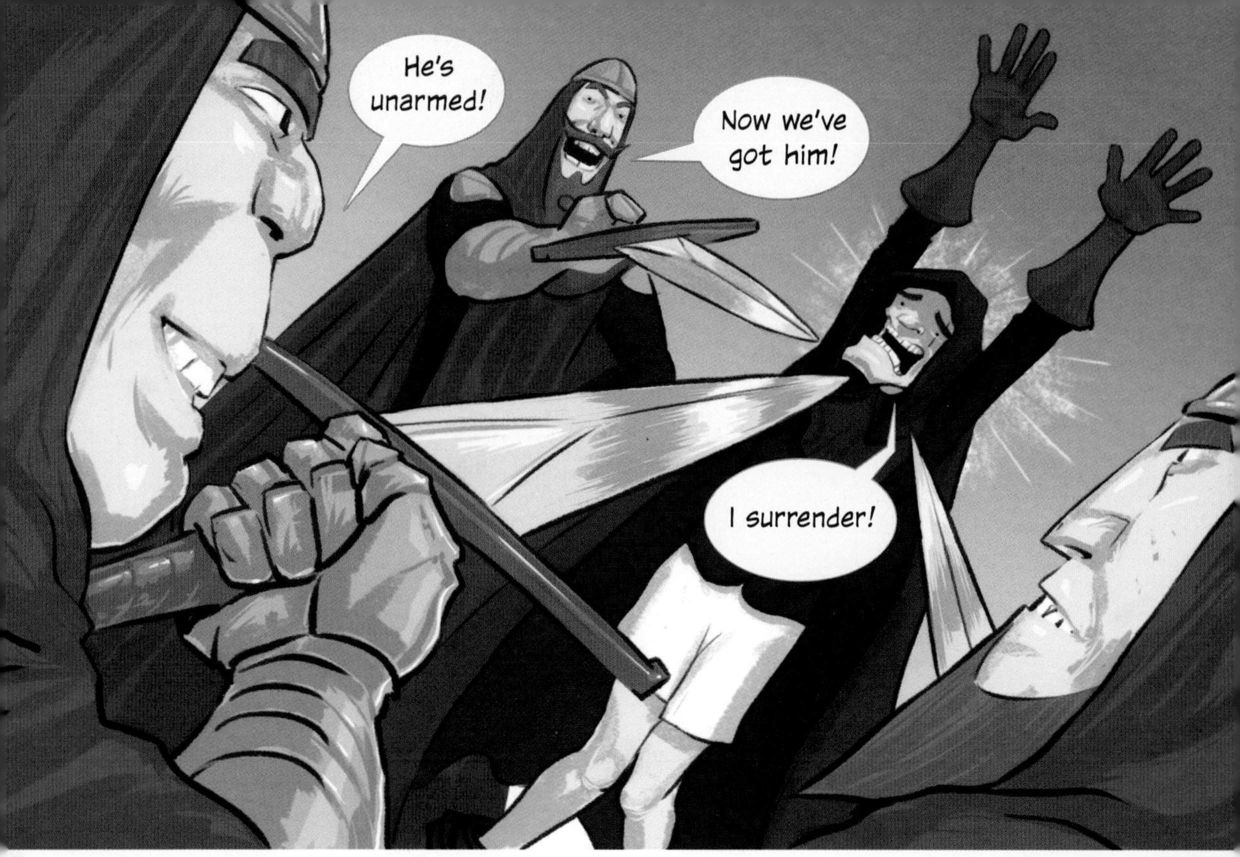
He's unarmed!
Now we've got him!
I surrender!

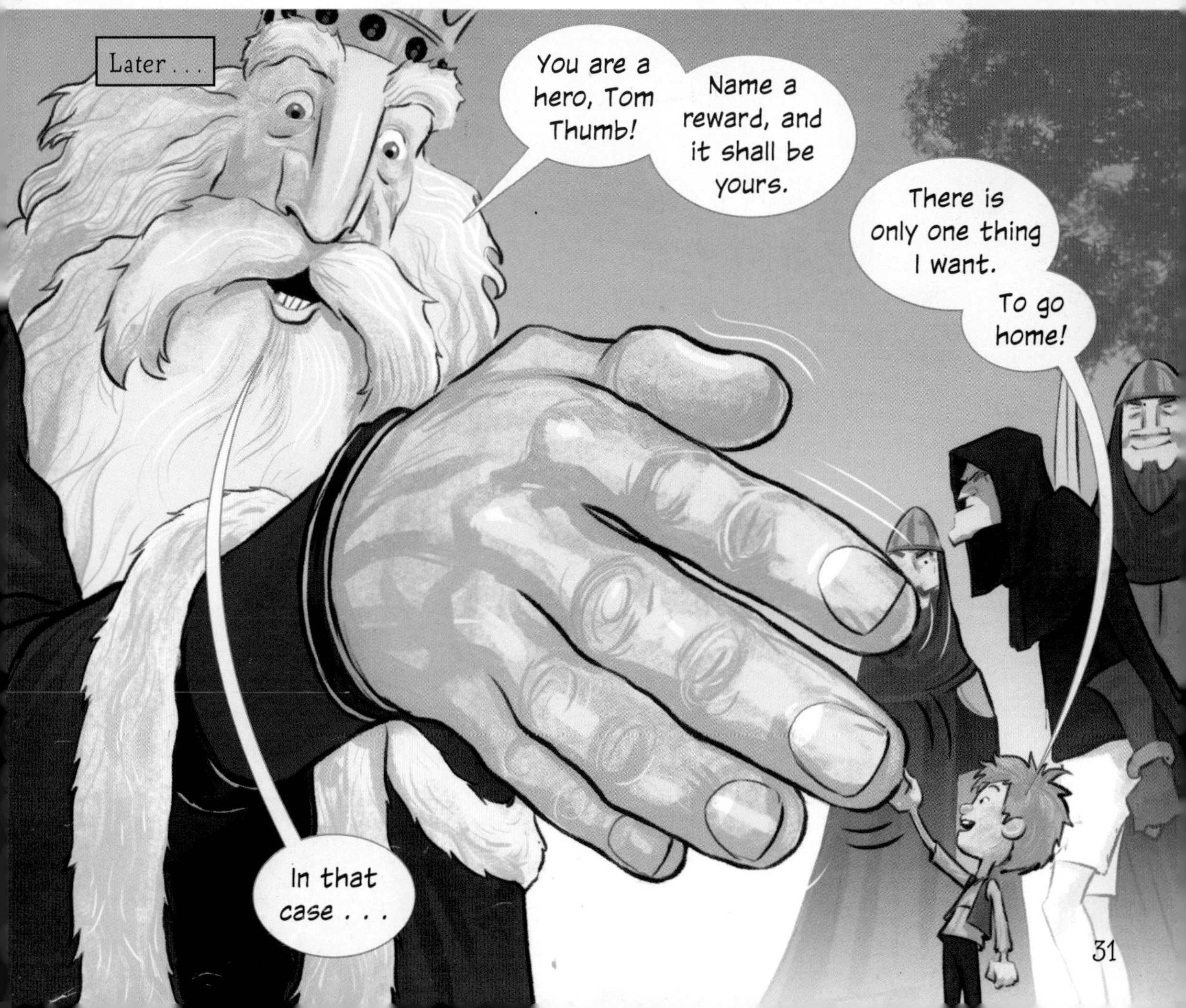
Later . . .
You are a hero, Tom Thumb!
Name a reward, and it shall be yours.
There is only one thing I want.
To go home!
In that case . . .

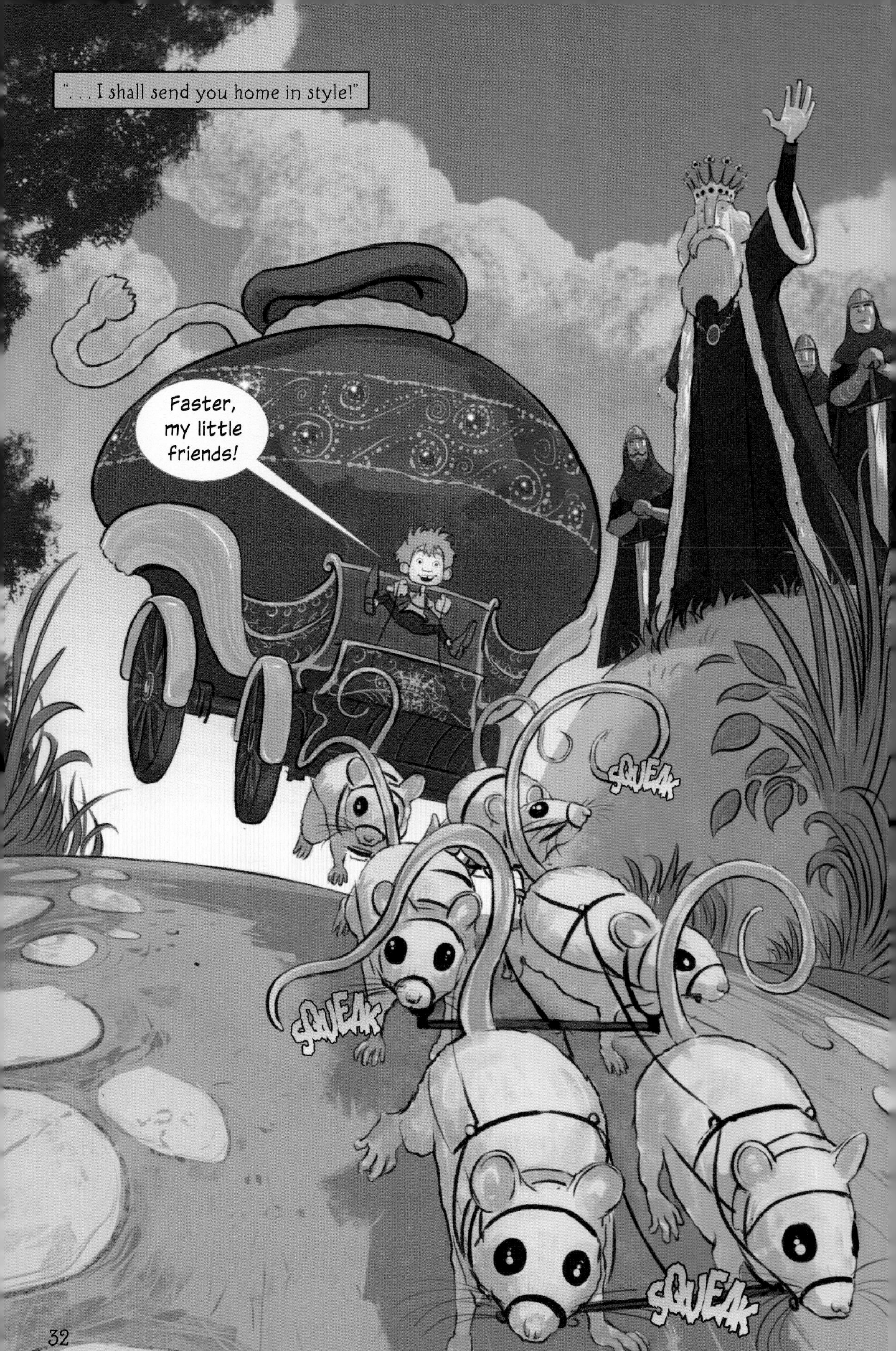
". . . I shall send you home in style!"
Faster, my little friends!
SQUEAK
SQUEAK
SQUEAK

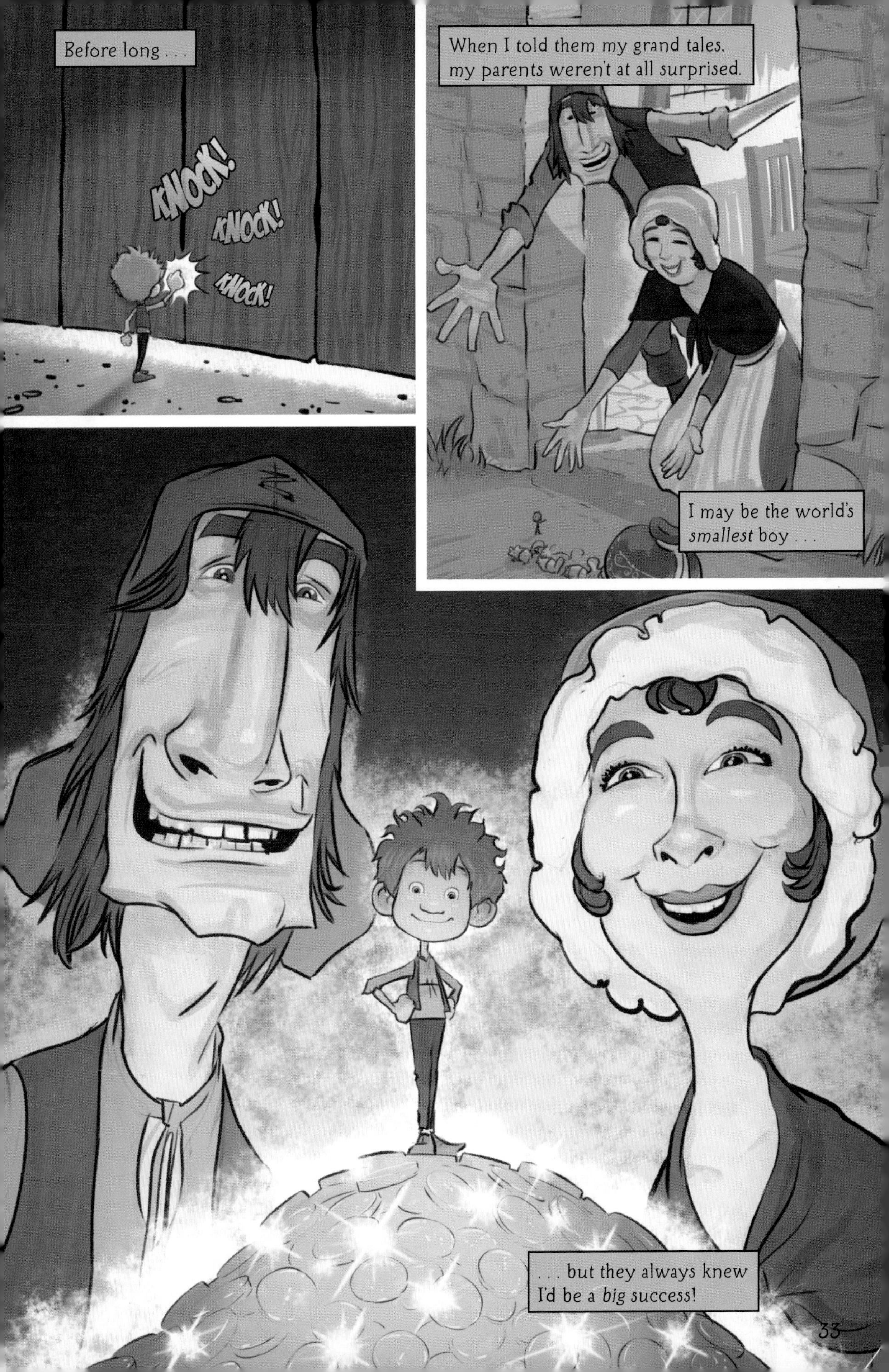
Before long . . .
KNOCK!
KNOCK!
KNOCK!
When I told them my grand tales, my parents weren't at all surprised.
I may be the world's *smallest* boy . . .
. . . but they always knew I'd be a *big* success!

THE BROTHERS GRIMM

A FAMILY OF FOLK AND FAIRY TALES

Jacob and Wilhelm Grimm were German brothers who invited storytellers to their home so they could write down their tales.

Peasants and villagers, middle-class citizens, wealthy aristocrats — even the Grimms' servants — contributed to their diverse collection of stories!

The brothers also collected folk tales from published works from other cultures and languages, adding to the variety of their sources.

In 1812, the Grimms published their collection of fairy tales, called *Children's and Household Tales.* The Brothers Grimm were among the first to collect and publish folk and fairy tales taken directly from the people who told them. These days, it would be hard to find anyone who hasn't at least heard of one of the Grimm Brothers' colorful characters!

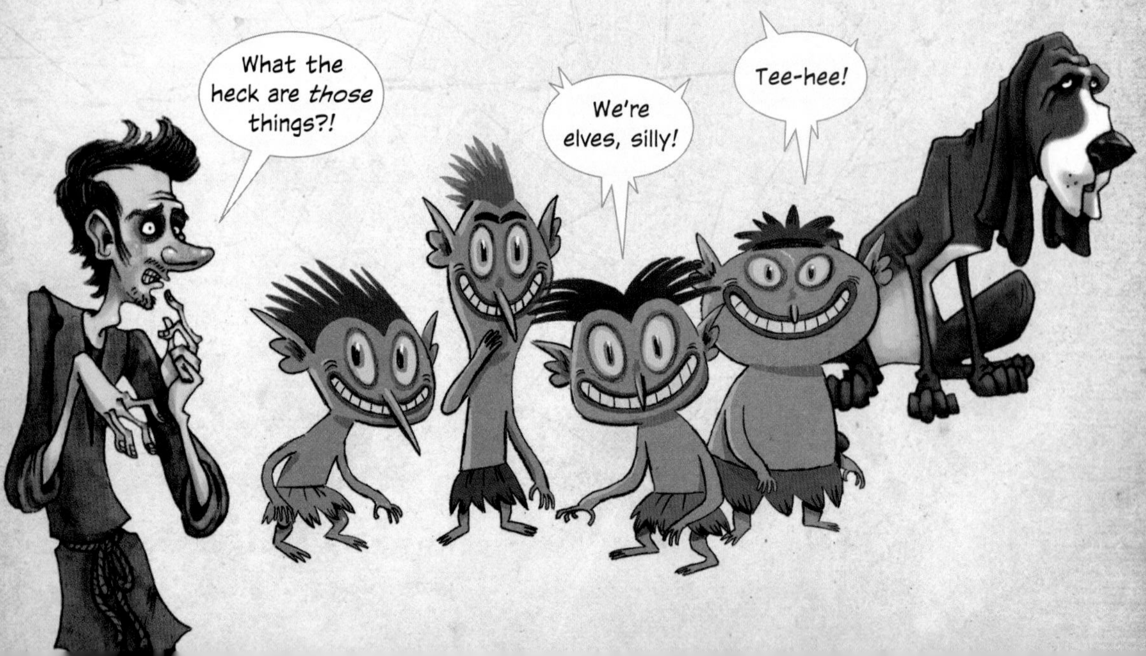
What the heck are *those* things?!
We're elves, silly!
Tee-hee!

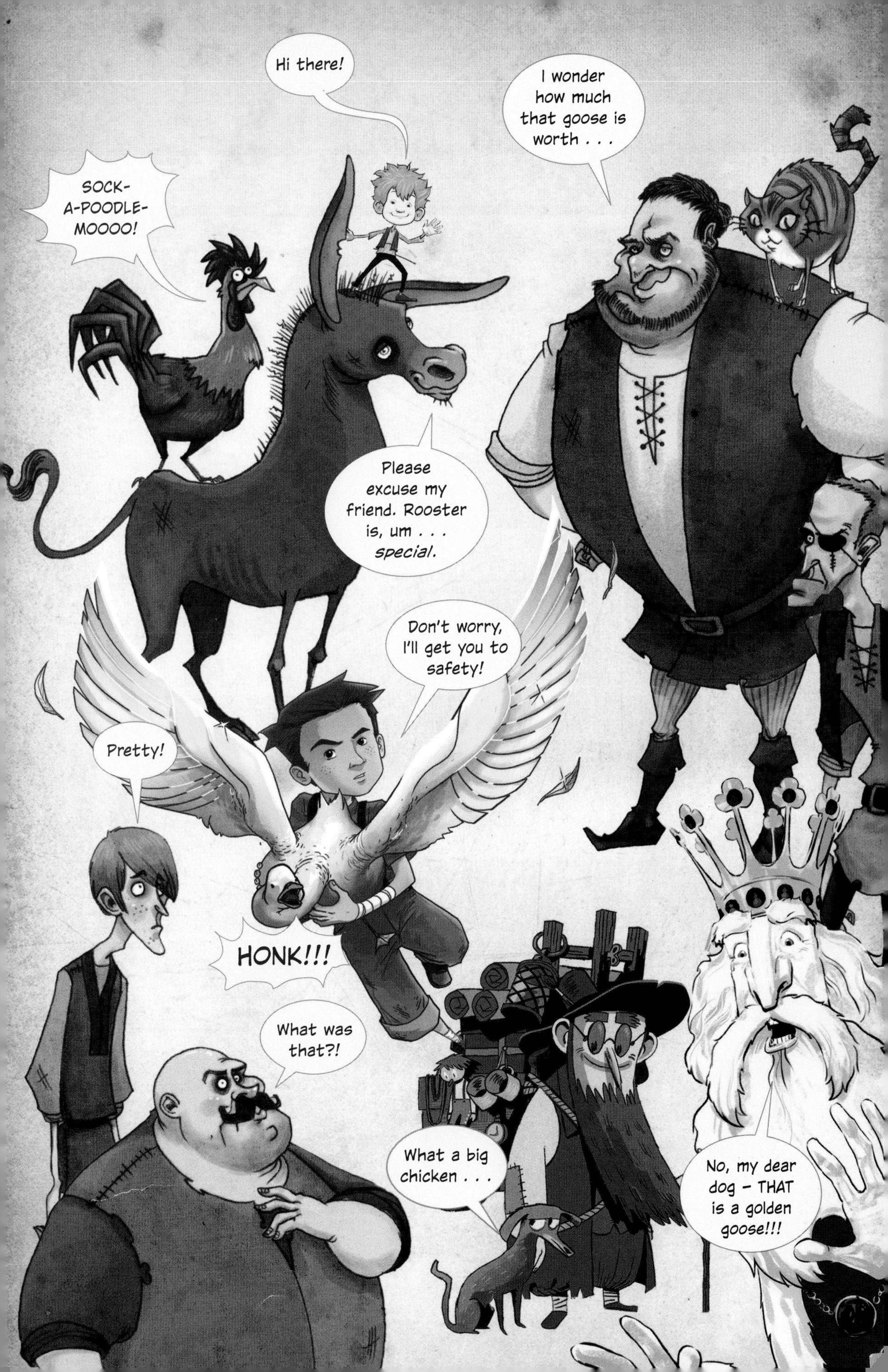
SOCK-
A-POODLE-
MOOOO!
Hi there!
I wonder how much that goose is worth . . .
Please excuse my friend. Rooster is, um . . . *special*.
Don't worry, I'll get you to safety!
Pretty!
HONK!!!
What was that?!
What a big chicken . . .
No, my dear dog – THAT is a golden goose!!!

ABOUT THE RETELLING AUTHOR

Scott Sonneborn has written 20 books, one circus (for Ringling Bros. Barnum & Bailey), and a bunch of TV shows. He's been nominated for one Emmy, and he spent three very cool years working at DC Comics. He lives in Los Angeles with his wife and their two sons.

ABOUT THE ILLUSTRATOR

Nelson Evergreen lives on the south coast of the United Kingdom with his partner and their imaginary cat. Evergreen is a comic artist, illustrator, and general all-around doodler of whatever nonsense pops into his head. He contributes regularly to the British underground comics scene, and is currently writing and illustrating a number of graphic novel and picture book hybrids for older children.

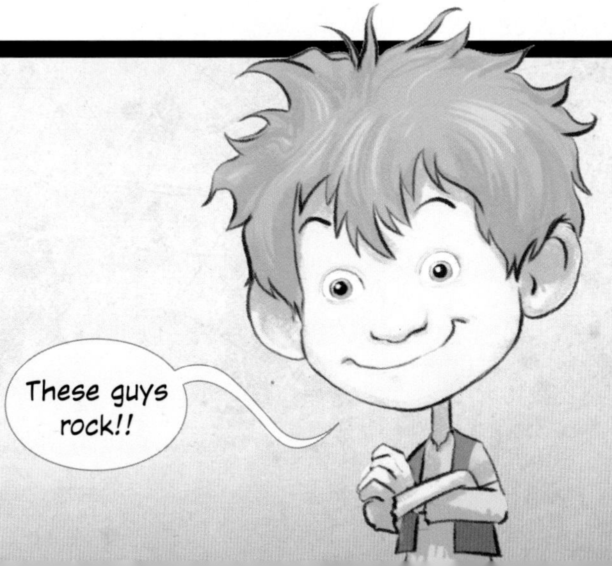
These guys rock!!

DISCUSSION QUESTIONS

1. Tom Thumb returns home with a large sack of gold coins. What would you buy with all that money? Talk about your purchases.

2. Tom Thumb faced many challenges because of his small size. What possible advantages could a tiny person have?

3. Which character in this book is your favorite? Why?

WRITING PROMPTS

1. Who helped Tom the most on his journey? If you had come across Tom while he needed help, what would you have done to get him back home safe and sound? Write about it.

2. The knights didn't think Tom could catch the rogue. Write about a time when someone said you couldn't do something, but you did it anyway.

3. Imagine that Tom Thumb gets lost in a city. What kinds of obstacles does he overcome to return home? Who does he meet? Write about Tom's new adventures.

GLOSSARY

ASTOUNDING (uh-STOUND-ing) — amazing or astonishing

CREATURE (KREE-chur) — a living being

DUEL (DOO-uhl) — a fight between two people involving swords or guns, fought according to strict rules

EMERGED (i-MURJD) — if you emerge from somewhere, you come out into the open

FOOL (FOOL) — a person who lacks good sense

GRAND (GRAND) — large and impressive

LOCALS (LOH-kuhlz) — the people or citizens who live in a city or town

ROGUE (ROHG) — a thief, bandit, or dishonest person

STRANGE (STRAYNJ) — unusual, odd, or unfamiliar

TERRORIZING (TER-uh-rize-ing) — frightening someone a great deal

VERMIN (VUR-min) — any of various small, common animals that are harmful pests

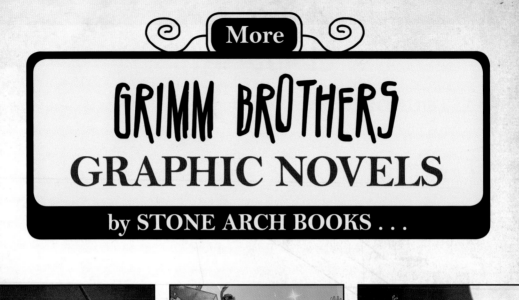